THE AMARNA AGE:BOOK 6

GUARDIAN
OF THE
UNDERWORLD

KYLIE QUILLINAN

First published in Australia in 2022.

ABN 34 112 708 734

kyliequillinan.com

A catalogue record for this book is available from the National Library of Australia.

Ebook ISBN: 9780645180084

Paperback ISBN: 9780645377194

Large print ISBN: 9781922852007

Hardback ISBN: 9781922852014

Audiobook ISBN: 9781922852021

This is a work of fiction. Any similarity between the characters and situations within its pages and places or persons, living or dead, is unintentional and coincidental.

Cover art by Deranged Doctor Design.

Edited by MS Novak.

Proudly independent. Please support indie authors by legally purchasing their work.

This work uses Australian spelling and grammar.

LP06062022

ONE

I am falling. Down. Down. The light is murky. My chest hurts. I am holding my breath.

I am not falling, but sinking.

The water envelopes me. It is cold and I can't hold my breath for much longer. Regret fills me at the knowledge that my child will never know her father.

I woke with tears in my eyes and a sob in my throat. I had experienced this event before, but by the time I was awake enough to wonder whether it was a dream or a memory, it had faded like waves rushing away from the shore.

The gentle rocking of the boat soon sent me back to sleep. For a time, my sleep was peaceful. Dreamless. Then an image appeared. A black scarab beetle, with blood dripping from its edges.

I woke with my heart pounding. It was a brand of some sort, burned into flesh. I had never seen such a thing, but it felt ominous. A warning perhaps. But I was tired after a long day of travel and the night was late. Guards stood at each end of the boat, their spears just as much a part of their silhouettes against the moonlit sky as their limbs. I was safe with them watching over us. Soon I fell asleep again.

When I next woke, the birds had begun their morning songs in anticipation of dawn, although the sky was still dark. Did my father and my brother watch over this next stage of my journey as I travelled from Memphis back to the island of Crete? Back to the underworld to retrieve Intef from the domain of Keeper of the Lake. But there were too many stars and if my loved ones were up there, I couldn't tell.

From the other end of the boat came soft snores I didn't recognise. Renni, Istnofret, Behenu and I had travelled together for so long that I knew the sounds of their sleep. The snorer could be Tuta, who used to be one of my guards, or Sabu from my brother's squad, who had both traveled with us. Or it could be one of ten other men, as we brought a full squad to guard us until we stepped onto the boat that would take us from Rhakotis to Crete. We weren't taking any chances with our safety this time. There were too many loose ends left here in Egypt. Too many men who might want to stop me.

The snores ceased and blankets rustled as someone — presumably the snorer — rolled over. I pulled my blanket up higher and closed my eyes, determined to get a little more sleep before the sun rose and we resumed our journey.

No sooner had I fallen asleep than the dreams returned. A confusing montage of images. Intef, Osiris, Keeper of the Lake. A young girl who displayed no emotion as Intef knelt in front of her and cried. Running through darkness with only a lamp for light, hot breath on my neck, fear coursing through my veins. The knowledge that we were being chased. No, hunted. *Be careful of the jackal. He is a trickster.* A row of baboons, seated on their haunches, looked at me with glittering eyes. The blood-dripping scarab. Something searched for me, not the beast that hunted me in the tunnels, but something else. I sank into deep water.

And woke with a gasp, choking as I tried to breathe, still not quite certain that air rather than water filled my lungs. I had to hold on to this memory long enough to understand it. But it slipped away, as it always did, and by the time I was properly awake, it was gone.

The girl who watched Intef as he cried must be our daughter, Meke-taten, who I gave to Osiris as payment for the Eye. She looked so much like the sister I named her for that I would recognise her anywhere. But she also had an otherworldly quality to her, something that suggested she wasn't quite of the mortal realm. Perhaps living in the underworld had changed her. Perhaps she wasn't fully mortal anymore.

Did my dream mean I would encounter her? She was only a few months old right now, so that event must be several years away. I tried to bury the thought and not let myself hope. She was the price I paid, and Osiris would never give her up. But at least I could look forward to the day when I would see her, even if it was only for a few minutes.

As for Intef, his agreement was with Keeper of the Lake, a minor deity at most. I could only pray that my dream of him with Meketaten didn't mean we would fail to convince Keeper to release him. Keeper had demanded a soul to stay as payment for the others passing through Anubis's gates. I didn't expect them to give up Intef any more than I thought Osiris would return Meketaten, but perhaps I could persuade Keeper to accept a new exchange. I planned to offer myself to secure Intef's release, although those who travelled with me didn't know.

There was no other option. We couldn't expect to retrieve Intef without some sort of payment and we couldn't leave him there forever. At least if I stayed, I might have the chance to see my daughter.

TWO

We were moored close to the bank of the Great River, out of the current's grasp, as the dawn sky came alight with an orange glow. The others stirred, first Renni, then Behenu, followed by Tuta, who seemed barely able to take his eyes off Behenu. Every time she stooped to pick up something, Tuta was there to pass it to her. When she reached for something, Tuta grabbed it for her.

Behenu cast him a few long looks, an expression of puzzlement on her face. As a slave, she had probably never expected such attention and even though she was a slave no longer, our journey to find the Eye and take it back to Egypt had left little time for anything else. I couldn't tell whether Tuta's attention pleased or confused her.

By the time Istnofret yawned and stretched, Behenu had laid out a meal. She called over the guards first so they could eat before they rowed us out into the middle of the Great River, where the current would carry us northwards. The rest of us would eat after the guards finished. We had plenty of supplies and could stop for more any time we needed. It was a strange position to be in after so many months where we often travelled with no more than we could carry.

Sabu walked between his men, talking to this one and that, no doubt arranging who would take which duties today. They ate quickly, so they could do the hard work of rowing before the day grew hot. It was mid *peret* now — the season of emergence when the waters that broke the banks of the Great River subsided, leaving behind the rich, black silt in which the farmers would plant their crops. Not the hottest time of year, but building up to that season.

Soon enough, we were out in the middle of the river. The guards set aside their oars and let the current push us along. The orange of dawn had faded into an endless blue sky and the movement of the boat made a pleasant breeze. I ate, then lay on my blanket, trying to come up with a way I might convince Keeper of the Lake to swap Intef for me. Distracted as I was, I was probably the last to realise something was wrong. It was the silence I noticed first — the sudden absence of the chatter that usually accompanies a group of travellers.

"What is it?" I asked, unable to see anything alarming from where I lay. They were all looking behind us.

Nobody responded, although Tuta glanced towards me and shook his head.

My heart already pounded a little harder as I got to my feet. If Tuta was worried, I should be too. Behind us was a boat. It was some distance away yet, too far to make out how many people it carried, or even whether it was bigger or smaller than ours.

"To your oars, men," Sabu said. "There's not much breeze to speak of, but rowing will move us faster than the current alone."

His squad moved quickly, with only a brief disagreement when two of the men wanted to sit in particular spots. Our boat picked up notice-able speed as they began to row.

"That will do it," Renni said as he came to stand beside me. "We surely have more men, so they won't be able to keep up, even if they row."

"Who is it?" I asked.

I shaded my eyes with my hand, but couldn't make out anything more than the merest suggestion of figures on board.

"I don't know." Renni's voice was terse. "But they were gaining rapidly, so whoever it is, they want to catch up to us."

"Do you think it is Khay?"

I had sentenced him to three years of labour in the Nubian slave mines for being a traitor and I would be unsurprised if he still sought revenge. We had encountered him when we first returned to Egypt, but lost him when I convinced the captain who imprisoned us at Khay's urging to let us go. That probably made him hate me even more.

"I don't know, and that is the truth," Renni said. "No point sitting around waiting to find out, though."

"But now we might never know who it is."

"Does it matter?"

I supposed not. Other than Intef and my sisters, everyone who mattered to me was on board this ship.

"How long can the men row?" I asked. "Won't whoever it is catch up when we stop rowing?"

Renni shot a glance towards the rowers.

"Our men will keep going for as long as they need to," he said. "Sabu, Tuta and I can spell them when they get too tired. We will outrun them."

"What if they don't give up? We will have to stop at night."

"We will row through the night if we need to. Our men are well trained, Samun, and very fit. They will row for as long as they must."

I studied his face. He looked out at the other boat, and although I couldn't read his expression, I was certain he was hiding something. He seemed too concerned about our pursuers to have no idea who they were.

"What are you not telling me, Renni?" I asked.

"What makes you say that?"

"I don't think we would make so much effort to outrun that boat if you didn't think you had good reason to be concerned."

"Something doesn't feel right," he said.

"Intef would tell you to trust your gut."

"And that is what I'm doing."

I jumped as Sabu called out.

"Steady on, men. Straighten her up a bit. We are headed towards the bank."

Our boat, which had been in the centre of the river, was now angled towards the shore.

"Steady, I said," Sabu yelled. "We will be up on that bank in no time at this rate."

The boat continued to veer towards the shore. Sabu strode along the deck, studying the rowers.

"You," he said, stopping beside one. "And you." A nod to the man behind. "We are off centre because you are not rowing hard enough."

I wasn't sure, but they might have been the two who made a fuss about wanting to take particular oars.

"Tired," one of the men said. "We have been rowing for too long."

"It has only been a few minutes," Sabu said. "You have trained much harder than you have worked today. Put your back into it."

"I woke up feeling unwell," the second man said. "I cannot row today."

"You don't row, you don't get paid." Sabu's tone was brusque now. "I have neither the time nor the patience for freeloaders. Either find the will to row harder or we will set you ashore the next time we stop. And you will not be paid before you leave."

Neither man responded, but they also didn't make much effort to row harder.

"Right," Sabu said. "Off the oars, both of you. You will disembark as soon as possible. You two" — he indicated two men on the other side of the boat — "leave your oars and come take over here. We need to straighten up before we drop out of the current."

The two men he called set aside their oars and came to stand beside the men they were to replace.

"Come on," one of them said. "Hurry up and move over."

The man only grunted. He had stopped rowing, but he didn't seem inclined to get up and let the other fellow in.

"Move," Sabu growled.

The man at the oar didn't even look at him, but cast his gaze off to the bank as if watching for something.

"Make him move," Sabu said, but before anyone could act, the other rower stood.

"I don't want any trouble," he said. "We were only supposed to delay the boat."

"Shut your mouth," the other fellow said, standing up as well.

"Sabu." Tuta's voice was terse.

He nodded behind us and we could all see the other boat gaining on us.

"We need to move," Renni said. "Get them out of the way and I will take an oar myself. Tuta, get over here."

Before anyone could move, the rower who said he didn't want any trouble jumped over board. He disappeared for a few moments, but then his head bobbed up above the water's surface. He moved his arms and seemed to actually know how to swim. Then he cried out and sank. I waited, barely able to breathe, but he didn't reappear.

"What happened?" I asked.

Surely no man could hold his breath under water for so long.

"Crocodile." Renni shrugged as he took up an oar.

"Or hippopotamus maybe." Tuta was already in position with the other oar. "Back to your spots, fellows," he said to the two men Sabu had called over. "We can still get back on course."

"He was a fool to jump in, as is any man who thinks to follow him." Sabu shot a fierce glare at the other troublesome rower. "Now, are you going to tell me what in the name of the gods is going on?"

The man shot an uneasy look towards the water and edged a little closer to the side of the boat.

"Tie him to the mast," Renni said. "We will deal with him when we get to Rhakotis. For now, let's worry about moving faster."

"It is too late," one of the other guards said. "They are upon us."

Our pursuers were now close enough that I could make out the figure who stood at the bow. It was Khay.

THREE

There was little time to prepare, for his boat was less than the length of a dozen men behind us. They were close enough that I could see Khay speaking, although the wind of our passage whipped his words away. He seemed animated, waving his arms as he yelled. Excited, or perhaps agitated at the possibility that we might once again slip out of his grasp.

Sabu yelled commands at his men. Intef would have been calmer. Giving orders, yes, but not flustered like Sabu. I pushed away the thought. It was unfair to Sabu, who could well be encountering his first armed engagement and undoubtedly his first as captain of a squad. Of course, Intef would react differently with his many years of experience.

One of Sabu's men grabbed my arm and led me to the bow where Istnofret and Behenu already waited. Another guard stood between them, his dagger held ready. Istnofret and Behenu also had their daggers in their hands. I fumbled for the pouch that should have been at my waist. Once again, I was the only one without my dagger. I had no time to dwell on it, for the spell bottle that hung on a cord around my neck suddenly burned, a coal against my chest. Then the boat rocked violently as our pursuers hit us from behind.

The movement flung me to my hands and knees. Blood filled my mouth as I bit my tongue. I spat out the blood and it splattered on the deck, its redness too bright against the dull wood. Would this be the first of many blood stains the deck would receive today?

Our guards had all left their oars by now and stood ready at the stern. One fellow let down an anchor. It seemed someone had decided we would stay and fight.

Sabu appeared to have given command over to Renni, who issued a stream of directions, telling this man to move over there and that man to cover Khay. He shot a glance back towards us women and nodded, seemingly satisfied we were safe enough.

Then Khay's boat drew up alongside us and our men set to work with their daggers, trying to keep his crew from coming aboard. The battle seemed to take a very long time, for Khay's men were determined and he most of all.

Even after he fell to his knees, Khay continued to swing his dagger, fending off two of Sabu's men at once. Two of his lay dead, blood pooling beneath them. Four others had surrendered and lay on their bellies, guarded by some of our men. Khay had brought little more than half a squad with him. Was this all the men he could entice with whatever riches and favour he had offered? And where did he get whatever he promised them? Surely he had little wealth of his own and not enough for such an endeavour.

At length, his dagger clattered to the deck, and Khay raised his hands in surrender. Tuta held his dagger to Khay's throat and looked at me.

"What are your orders, my lady?" he asked.

I came forward to stand in front of Khay. He met my eyes, his gaze neither remorseful nor beseeching.

"Do you have anything to say for yourself?" I asked.

It seemed wrong to kill an unarmed man as he knelt in front of me. But Khay glared up at me and spat on the deck.

"You are an abomination," he hissed. "May the gods ruin your house."

I tried not to flinch at his curse.

"You told me once that a traitor should never be allowed to live," I said. "Should we consider you anything other than a traitor?"

He spat again.

"We should deal with him now, my lady," Renni whispered in my ear. "Before he has opportunity to escape."

"Should we not interrogate him first?" I asked. "He might have information that would be useful to us. It would, at least, be helpful to know who is financing him."

"I can try, but I doubt he will give us anything useful. All Intef's men learned interrogation techniques, both how to do it and how to withstand it. He knows everything I do. If he gives us anything, it will not be the truth."

I hardened my heart and tried not to dwell on another life lost because of me. Khay deserved none of my pity.

"Kill him," I said to Tuta.

The words were barely out of my mouth before Tuta's dagger moved.

Blood spurted and Khay made a noise that might have been a groan of pain or perhaps just a gurgle. He slumped to the deck and in moments his gaze stilled.

As I stared down at Khay's body, I tried to make sense of the emotions that filled me. Satisfaction that he had finally paid for his treachery. Sadness at knowing the man Intef once considered his brother had gone to the West. Bitterness that I used to trust this man almost as much as I trusted Intef.

"My lady." Tuta gestured to the four men who had surrendered. "What do you wish done with them?"

I looked at each of them. If I was to sentence them to death today, I wanted to at least take the time to look them in the eyes. But when I reached the fourth man, my breath caught in my throat. It was Nebamun. The man my ladies once suggested I take as my lover and who Intef had suspected of sending his cousin to kill me. Now I knew where Khay's riches likely came from. Nebamun met my gaze and I took a step back at the hatred in his glare.

"You tried to kill me merely because I didn't take you to my bed?" I asked.

"You humiliated me," he snarled.

"Nobody knew other than the guards who were there that night and my ladies."

Nebamun swallowed down a reply. He, it seemed, had told others. He must have been very certain of himself, but I had promised nothing more than a meal.

"Was coming after me your idea or Khay's?" I asked.

Nebamun didn't reply.

"Do you really hate me that much?"

"They are all traitors," Renni said. "Their motives are irrelevant. We cannot afford to let any of them go. Not unless you want to spend the rest of your life looking over your shoulder. We don't know the depth of their allegiance to Khay. They may seek vengeance for his death, even if they don't have their own reasons for pursuing you."

"Their allegiance wasn't deep enough to stop them from surrendering," I said.

But having already ordered the death of one man today, another four came more easily. I didn't stay to watch as Nebamun died.

FOUR

Restoring order to the boat took some time. We dropped the dead men's bodies into the Great River, and I wondered whether the crocodile-headed god Sobek and Taweret, who often took the form of a hippopotamus, would find their corpses an acceptable offering.

We scrubbed the blood from the deck, using fresh water drawn from the river. The coppery aroma lingered even after Behenu sprinkled herbs over the deck to mask the odour. One guard had a deep gash to the side of his trunk, but thankfully this was the worst of the injuries to our men. None of those who defended us were killed or permanently maimed. It seemed Khay chose his party for their enthusiasm for his cause, rather than their skills.

There was some debate about what to do with the other boat, which was still wedged up against ours, held there by its anchor and the force of the current. Tuta suggested sending a few men to row it to shore, but Renni and Sabu wanted to avoid any further delay. In the end, we left it where it was.

"I suppose someone will claim it sooner or later," Renni said.

"Do you think anyone else will come after us?" I asked.

"Who can say? You have made a lot of enemies. Perhaps we should hire more guards."

"But they will be strangers to us. Are we not safer with Sabu's men?"

"Two of Sabu's men turned out to be traitors."

Sabu seemed to feel Renni's hard stare from the other end of the boat. He acknowledged Renni with a nod. The second troublesome rower had disappeared during the fighting. Perhaps he, too, had jumped overboard.

"If men handpicked by someone we trust can be traitors, our odds with a stranger are probably much the same," Renni said. "I am inclined to take our chances with more men."

I turned away with a shrug, not wanting to argue with him. I was certain to my core we shouldn't trust anyone who wasn't already on the boat with us, but that was a discussion we could have later. For now, I only wanted to be away from here.

Nobody spoke much for the rest of the day. The men carried out their tasks in silence, although I noticed their frequent glances behind us. Sabu now had a guard assigned to do nothing but watch our surroundings as we sailed, something he had previously done only when we stopped at night.

We women sat together at the bow where we were mostly out of the way of the working men. Blood still oozed from my tongue and I got up now and then to spit it into the water. Behenu checked my mouth and said it was only a deep cut which would stop bleeding soon enough. She seemed absorbed in her thoughts after that, but Istnofret picked at a stray thread on her skirt, a sure sign something troubled her. I let her be and didn't ask. She would tell me what was on her mind sooner or later. Probably sooner.

"Where do you think Tentopet is?" she asked at length.

"She wasn't on the boat with Khay," I said.

"We could all see that. So where is she?"

"Somewhere else. Does it matter?"

Istnofret picked at the thread some more.

"I just wondered. It seems strange that Khay looked after her for so long, but left her alone now."

"He probably didn't plan to go to the West today," I said. "I suppose she is at their home, wherever it is."

"She might be waiting for him to come home and will never know what happened to him."

"She deserves none of your sympathy," I said, probably a little too harshly. "She is a traitor."

"She is also a woman wondering what happened to her man."

I gave Istnofret a hard look.

"Then go find her if it bothers you that much," I said. "You can take news of Khay's fate to her. Meanwhile, I will go to Crete and find Intef."

Istnofret gave a heavy sigh.

"You misunderstand me," she said. "I didn't say I wanted to go find her. I merely felt sorry that she will never know what happened to him."

"She will probably guess," Behenu said.

I hadn't thought she was listening.

"She likely knew what he was going to do today," Behenu continued. "When he doesn't return, she will figure it was because he was defeated."

"There you go, Ist," I said. "Behenu is right. You can rest easy and not feel sorry for Tentopet."

Istnofret gave a little shrug and turned away. She pretended she watched something on the shore for a while, but soon got up and wandered off. I let her go without comment. It wasn't the first time Istnofret had spoken kindly of Khay and it made me wonder just how well I really knew her.

FIVE

We reached Rhakotis the following morning. From here, we would sail to Crete.

"I think you should keep out of sight until we are on the ship," Istnofret said to Renni. "They might still be looking for you. They will arrest you if they recognise you."

"I doubt they still watch for me after all these months," Renni said. "Besides, I have to sell the boat."

"There are others who can do that."

"Tuta is going to find us transport to Crete and Sabu will be busy with his men. I said I would take care of the boat."

"I will do it then," Istnofret said. "Tell me how."

"Ist, I can look after it. I will take a couple of guards with me. Even if someone recognises me, it will take time for him to secure enough backup to take on all of us. We will have time to figure out a plan."

"You are being ridiculous. There is no reason for you to take such a risk. Send one of Sabu's men if you must, but you should stay here until Tuta finds a way to get us to Crete."

"Ist, please," Renni started, but she threw up her arms with a huff.

"Samun, you tell him," she said crossly. "He will not listen to reason from me."

No matter who I supported, one of them would be unhappy with me.

"I am not getting involved," I said.

Istnofret shot me a dirty look and Renni seemed little happier. I tried to avoid both of them as we piled our packs in a shady patch of dirt with two men to guard them. We could replace everything easily enough if necessary, for we had numerous jewels secreted away amongst Renni, Istnofret, Behenu and me, but it would take time and that was the one thing we couldn't replace.

Every day we spent here was another day Intef passed in the underworld, assuming time ran the same there as it did here. Perhaps a day to us was a month to him, or a year, or a century. We had no way of knowing. He looked no older when I saw him in my dreams — the true dreams that foretold outcomes of my decisions — but that didn't mean time had stopped passing for him.

Renni departed to sell the boat, taking two guards with him. Istnofret huffed and stomped around, but Renni only gave her a sorrowful look and walked away.

Tuta left to find a ship with a captain willing to sail with only us onboard. Since the captain would know the kind of wealth we carried, or he would at least suspect there must be more than we paid him, we had decided Sabu's squad would accompany us to Crete. They would then come back to Egypt and be free to either return to Memphis or go somewhere else. Renni had talked again about hiring more guards, but he was the only one in favour of it and he let the matter drop.

Istnofret, Behenu and I waited with the guards who stood over our packs. The rest of the men busied themselves with cleaning the boat and preparing her for her new owner. Renni returned in less than an hour. I would have thought that was far too fast for him to have sold the boat, but he beamed.

"I made the sale," he said. "And I ran into Mahu."

"I did not expect to see him again," I said.

Istnofret only huffed, although I wasn't sure whether she intended it as a comment on Mahu or as a reminder that she was still mad at Renni.

Mahu had been locked in the same cell as Renni and escaped with him when we women broke through the back wall of the prison. When he, Renni and Behenu went back to retrieve the pack containing the Eye, Mahu distracted the prison guards long enough for Renni and Behenu to get away, which resulted in him being captured again. Once I claimed the throne, Renni arranged for his release, which was fortunate for Mahu, who had been sentenced to labour in the Nubian slave mines.

"He wants to come with us to Crete," Renni said.

"Why?" I asked.

"I suppose he feels he owes you a debt for saving him from the mines," Renni said. "Also, I think he sees this as some grand adventure. He has probably never done anything important before, not with his illness. Maybe he thinks it is a chance to do something worthy."

"We hardly know him," Istnofret said. "I know he helped you in Rhakotis, but what do we know about him other than that he cannot hold down a job and steals to survive? He is not an honourable man."

"Ist." Renni shot her a disapproving look. "He allowed himself to be captured so Behenu and I could get away. If that doesn't show he is honourable, then I don't know what evidence would satisfy you."

"He is a thief and a liar," Istnofret said.

"Have any of us done nothing of which we are not proud?" Renni asked. "Ist, can you honestly say there is not a single thing you regret? That you have done nothing that is less honourable than you would wish it to be?"

She frowned at him. "You know I have, and you know how I felt about it."

I wondered whether she meant the man she killed, although she had done it to save her virtue and possibly her life. Surely she didn't consider that to be a dishonourable act.

"How can you compare me to Mahu?" she asked. "You know me. You hardly know him."

"I know enough to be certain we can trust him," Renni said. "Behenu, will you back me up?"

Behenu darted glances between them and seemed to weigh who she should side with.

"When we were trying to get away," she said, "I tripped, and a guard landed on top of me. I tried to stab him, but my hands shook so much that I only stabbed myself. Mahu smacked the man in the back of the head with his dagger. The man fell off me and I ran away."

She had never told us how she came to be stabbed that day. Renni had said Mahu helped them escape, but I never knew he intervened to save Behenu. Thank the goddess I told Renni to arrange for Mahu's release before I went to the palace to confront Ay. By the time I had the power to do such a thing myself, I was too far under the Eye's spell to care. Istnofret said nothing else about not wanting Mahu to come and I figured the decision had been made.

The day passed slowly while we waited for Tuta. I told myself to be patient. That he needed to find a captain who didn't already have pressing business elsewhere and was willing to be diverted. He might even have to wait for other ships to arrive, other captains to come onshore. We could be here for a few days yet.

But Tuta returned shortly before sunset with news that he had found a captain willing to depart at dawn, provided the weather was suitable. The man had previously lost a ship, most of his crew, and very nearly his own life in a storm, and was unwilling to take any chances if there was even the slightest sign of the weather turning. Renni slipped away to tell Mahu where to meet us.

We found accommodation for the night and I slept restlessly, tormented by dreams of sinking down into deep water. When we woke, the sky was clear and a light breeze promised to chase away any clouds. We arrived at the dock to find the captain already preparing to sail. After stowing our packs down below, we gathered on the deck.

"Isn't it wonderful to not have to hide below in the dark?" Istnofret tipped her head back to let the sunlight fall fully on her face.

"I don't know why we didn't think to hire a ship to ourselves earlier," I said.

"I suppose the journey from Rhakotis to Crete is one thing," she said. "It is only a few days, after all. Maybe it would not be possible to find someone willing to take us all the way to Indou."

I supposed she was right. Not that it mattered now. This was likely our final sea voyage, or at least the last one for all of us together. Istnofret and Renni intended to stay in Crete once our mission was complete and Behenu would probably go home to Syria.

As for me, I would spend the rest of my life in the underworld, assuming we convinced Keeper to release Intef. He might want to stay in Crete with Istnofret and Renni, or he might choose to go back to Egypt alone. Either way, I would ensure he had both his share of the gems and mine. It wasn't like I would need riches in the underworld.

SIX

Mahu was pale and sweating when he arrived and with only minutes to spare before the captain announced he was ready to sail. He bowed to me, then went off to find somewhere to sit without saying a word.

"That was strange," I muttered to Istnofret.

"He looks very unwell," she said. "Perhaps he should not be travelling today."

But the ship started to leave the dock, and it was too late to suggest that Mahu stay in Rhakotis. Our journey to Crete was uneventful. We spent much of it studying a copy of the Book of the Amduat — or Book of the Underworld — to prepare for the journey ahead of us. We lay the scroll on the deck and pinned down the edges with various items from our packs so the wind wouldn't rip it away.

According to the Book, the underworld consisted of twelve sections and I tried to memorise each of them. The hole in the tunnels might lead us to a different part of the underworld this time. Scattered throughout the Book were spells and helpful hints, and perhaps we would need one of them in order to navigate our way through that place. Perhaps some clue hidden within these images would be the key to retrieving Intef. I fought down a rising tide of panic that I wouldn't be able to remember everything.

The Book contained the names and images of various gods and goddesses of the underworld and I did my best to learn them all. Amongst the images I found two leonine figures. Beneath one was a neat label with her name: Invoked by the Two Lands. The other had no label. Was this Keeper? Even if it was, there was no information about them, just a sketch of a lion-headed figure.

I studied the images of the Judgment of the Dead. Osiris presided over the events from his throne, accompanied by a line of baboon sentinels and the forty-two judges. Anubis weighed the heart of the deceased, while Ammut, the Devourer, waited to feast on any heart that was too heavy. Thoth recorded the results on a scroll. I spent hours poring over this section. The baboons looked just like the ones in my dream, so perhaps I would meet Osiris again. I tried not to think about the fact that if I were to face judgement, it would be because I had died. I knew all too well how I might die on this journey.

I couldn't find any reference to the Gates of Anubis through which we had accessed the Lake of Fire, which was our path back to the world of the living last time. There were no descriptions of other ways to return to our world, but the Book was intended for the souls of the deceased who had no need to do anything other than navigate the underworld. I had to trust there would be another way for my friends to return if they couldn't go through the Lake of Fire again.

Eight days later, the Cretan coastline appeared and we reached it by midafternoon. The last time we arrived in Crete, Intef was at my side and our babe still in my belly. I always knew I would give Osiris my babe at some point, but I had thought that would occur in Egypt. Leaving Crete without either Intef or our babe had never seemed possible.

Thinking about Crete reminded me of my shadow. Despite my promise to speak to it, I often forgot for days or even weeks at a time. I never meant to. I supposed I should try harder, but it was a difficult thing to remember to speak to something that could never reply.

"Shadow, can you hear me? I wonder if we will be able to communicate again when we reach the underworld? I suppose you are angry I keep forgetting you. Angry I have separated you from your mate."

My shadow seemed as bonded to Intef's shadow as I was to the man himself. I didn't mention my shadow's babe, who must have stayed in the underworld with Meketaten. I couldn't imagine my shadow had any fond feelings for me right now.

"We have lots to talk about if we get the chance."

I had no time to dwell further on my shadow as we drew into the harbour and prepared to disembark. The captain intended to spend the night onshore before returning to Rhakotis in the morning. We farewelled our guards, who would depart with him, and gave them their payments. They had each been promised a gem for transporting us safely and all seemed well pleased with what they received.

We had hoped to hire the house we occupied last time, but when Behenu went to enquire with the owners, they had already let it out. However, they directed her to a place called a *caravanserai*, which seemed to be a kind of public bathing house. It had no sleeping accommodations, but we could at least rest for a while and soak our feet. Mahu sat a little away from the rest of us. He hadn't spoken much as we sailed. Perhaps he was still unwell, or maybe he regretted coming with us. I barely knew him, though, and didn't feel like I could ask.

"Someone will have to make enquiries about a house," Istnofret said. "It is almost sunset, so we do not have much time."

"We can find somewhere to camp for tonight," Renni said. "We have done that often enough. The weather looks fine and we were only planning to stay here one night before we head to the ruins."

"It has been a while since we slept outdoors," Istnofret said, a little ruefully. "I think I have gotten too soft to cope with such a thing. I am really longing for a proper bath after a week at sea."

"At least we have clean feet." Behenu grinned as she kicked water at Istnofret.

I smiled as Istnofret splashed her back, heartened to see them in such good spirits. Behenu was always cheeriest when she was on or near the water, but it confused me that Istnofret didn't seem happier. After all, this was the place she had fallen in love with and never wanted to leave. Shouldn't she be happy to be back?

We left the *caravanserai* and made our way down the beach until we were out of sight of anyone at the harbour.

"We should have kept the guards overnight," Istnofret said. "They are not leaving until tomorrow, anyway."

"We will have someone on guard duty as we always do," Renni said. "There are plenty of us to share that task without anyone losing too much sleep. It is only one night."

I would have felt comfortable enough with Renni, Tuta, Sabu and Mahu to guard us, but Istnofret's unease rubbed off on me. I slept restlessly and kept waking with a start. I dreamed about Meketaten. She was some distance away from me and I could only just make her out, but I knew it was her. She seemed to say something I couldn't hear.

I sat up for a while, wrapped in my blanket and wide awake. Whatever had woken me was gone now. Perhaps a bird had squawked or something rustled a nearby bush. The dream about Meketaten couldn't be a true dream. I had seen no alternative version. Perhaps it was no more than a reflection of my longing to see her again. To speak with her.

The moon was full tonight and the waves glistened in its light. Their restlessness made me uneasy as they drew away from the shore, then rushed back in again, inviting me to come out to them. To sink down into their embrace.

The water was cold and deep. I cradled my belly, filled with sorrow and regret. My babe would never know her father. Eventually I could hold my breath no more and I opened my mouth. Water rushed in, filling my lungs.

I woke gasping. I had fallen asleep sitting up. I lay back down and pulled my blanket over my head, trying to drown out the sound of the waves.

SEVEN

The following morning, Tuta found an Egyptian fellow willing to transport us to the ruins. He had a large cart and two oxen, and didn't seem to be in any particular hurry. He leaned against the twisted trunk of a tamarisk and made no move to help as we loaded our baggage.

"I think we brought too much," Behenu said as she dragged a heavy basket over to the cart.

Tuta swooped in and lifted the basket with exaggerated ease. Behenu gave him a bemused look.

"Perhaps we can leave some of it at the entrance to the tunnels," Tuta said, setting the basket in the cart. "One of us could stay to guard them."

I had told none of them about my dream. The one in which the beast hunted us through the tunnels and someone fell, only to be eaten. It would be me or one of the others, but I didn't know who. Guilt gnawed at me for not telling them, but how many would refuse to come with me if I did? I would likely need their help to find Intef and I didn't know what condition he would be in after spending so long in the under-world. He might need help to get home. I couldn't afford to tell them.

"We should stay together," I said. "I am sure there will be somewhere safe enough to leave the things we don't need."

"We could hire someone to watch them," Istnofret said. "Surely someone who lives nearby would appreciate some easy work."

We finished loading the cart and squeezed ourselves in as well. I pitied the poor oxen even as I was grateful we wouldn't have to walk so far. I was wedged between Istnofret and Behenu. Their bodies were too warm and Istnofret's elbow dug into my ribs. I tried to get more comfortable, but there really was no room, and I resigned myself to a disagreeable journey. The cart's owner settled himself on the front seat, clicked at his oxen, and we set off.

The path was rougher than I remembered, although I recognised some of what we passed. That oak tree, its broad branches shading a child's swing made from a plank and some rope. A cottage, small and not particularly well maintained. A woman stood in the doorway, watching us pass. I raised my hand in greeting, but she only stared stonily, leaving me feeling a little foolish. Some time later, the cart came to an abrupt halt.

"There you go," its owner said.

He remained seated while we unloaded our packs. My body was stiff after the journey, and although I tried to help, I probably just got in everyone's way. Renni handed the man the basket of supplies we had agreed as payment.

"We should have asked him to stay and watch our packs," Behenu said as the cart trundled away.

"Well, he is gone now," Istnofret said. "A shame nobody thought of that earlier."

"I could watch them," Mahu offered. "I am neither fast nor strong, and I am probably the least useful person here."

"There are some homes not too far away." Tuta nodded towards a cluster of cottages. "We could try to hire someone from there. The morning is late enough that anyone able to labour will already be gone for the day, but there will surely be an old person or even a child. All they need to do is sit in the shade and watch our packs."

"Go on," Renni said. "See if you can hire someone while we find what we need to take down into the tunnels. Mahu, you can stay behind if Tuta can't find a volunteer, but if he can, I think we should all go. It is never a bad thing to have an extra man you can trust."

Tuta set off at a slow jog and I finally turned to look at the ruins. This had been a grand palace once, easily the size of the one I grew up in. I tried to imagine what it might have looked like before the earthquakes that destroyed it, but all I could see were images from my childhood. Mud brick walls covered with bright murals. Large windows letting in both light and breeze. A square pond. Potted plants. Mosaics on the floors. It had been a long time since I thought of my childhood home of Akhetaten, my father's desert city. My heart ached at the thought, although not quite as strongly as it once would have. Time had dulled both the pain and the memories.

"Samun?"

I pushed away the images and gave Istnofret a small smile.

"Just thinking," I said.

"Of Akhetaten?"

It never failed to amaze me how she always knew exactly what was on my mind.

"I was trying to imagine what the palace might have looked like before, but all I could see was Akhetaten," I said.

"It must have been a fine place indeed." Istnofret shaded her eyes as she looked out at the ruins. "You can see glimpses of it here and there. A column with some paint on it. A bit of wall that still stands. The colours in the broken floor tiles. It would have been a beautiful place to live."

"I wonder what happened to the people who lived here. I know the palace was destroyed too long ago for them to still be alive, but I wonder where they went afterwards."

"Maybe they lived nearby." Istnofret cast a glance behind us. "Not those cottages there. They are not old enough. But maybe they built new homes here somewhere."

"Why would they build a cottage when they had lived in a palace?"

She shrugged. "I would rather think they lived in cottages than…"

Her voice trailed away, but I knew what it was she didn't want to say. The people who lived here probably didn't survive the palace's destruction. Maybe the palace buried them as it fell. Some people said the underworld could only be accessed through a tomb. We had previously wondered whether the tunnels might be such a place.

I tried to cast away my thoughts of folk buried beneath the ruined palace as Tuta returned with an old man. His head was bald and his back so stooped that he walked almost doubled over. He leaned on a wooden cane and gave us a cheerful, and entirely toothless, grin.

"He speaks no Egyptian, but I think he understands me well enough," Tuta said.

He gave Renni a questioning look, as if asking whether the man was suitable, but Renni just shrugged. Tuta guided the old man over to a tree and helped him to sit where he could lean against the trunk. They seemed to have a conversation of sorts, which involved much waving of hands from Tuta and enthusiastic nods from the old man.

"I don't think he understands anything Tuta says," Behenu said quietly.

"It is unlikely that anyone here speaks Egyptian," Renni said. "Or even Akkadian. We will have to trust he understands enough to not abscond with our things as soon as we leave."

"I offered to stay," Mahu said.

"No, we might need you," Renni said. "Tuta would not have brought the fellow if he didn't think he had managed to communicate enough to him."

While we waited for Tuta, Renni had sorted through our packs and made two piles: the things we would take down into the tunnels and those we would leave here. The packs we were taking seemed to be a much larger pile, but between us, we managed to carry them all. No wonder Renni wanted Mahu to come. We would have to leave something behind otherwise.

"Ready?" Renni asked once we were all weighed down with packs.

Just as we were about to set off, the old man shouted. He pointed at me.

"What do you think he is saying?" Istnofret asked.

"I have no idea, but it is something about Samun," Renni said.

"You should go to him," Behenu said to me. "See what he wants. Maybe he has information that might be useful in the tunnels."

"Even if he does, I won't be able to understand him," I said. "And I have never seen him before. How could he have any information for me?"

But they all agreed it was definitely me the old man wanted. I set down my packs and went to him. When I crouched in front of him, he looked me in the eye for a long moment, then reached for me. I took his hand hesitantly.

His skin was dry and brittle, like the old papyrus scrolls in the archives in Babylon. He clasped my hand with a grip that was unexpectedly firm, given his apparent frailness. He didn't speak, only pointed behind me with his other hand. I turned to look, still trapped by his grip.

In front of one of the cottages stood a woman who appeared to be even older than him. I couldn't make out her expression from this distance, but I got the sense that she waited. For me.

I turned back to the old man and he nodded towards her. As I got to my feet, he continued to grasp my hand, only reluctantly letting go when I pulled away. I returned to the others.

"He wants me to go to her." I pointed towards the woman.

"We don't have time for this," Renni said. "Too much of the day has passed as it is and we haven't even made it to the tunnels yet. Maybe you can go see her when we return."

"The tunnels are dark either way," I said. "Does it matter whether we enter them during the day or at night?"

"Don't forget the beast Renni and I heard about," Behenu said. "The priests told us it has lived there for many years. I think we would be better going into the tunnels during the day."

I flinched before I could stop myself and prayed nobody noticed my reaction.

"We saw no sign of any such beast last time, Behenu," Renni said quickly. "Even if such a creature lived there once, it would not still be alive all these years later."

"It could be," Behenu said. "Or it might have bred. There could be a whole family of them down there by now. A pack of beasts."

"If there was a pack of beasts, we would have seen something," Renni said. "Excrement. Remains of their food. Some sign that something used those passages. Remember how dusty they were? If any such beast lived down there, we would have noticed."

Behenu shrugged, seemingly unconvinced.

"Such stories do not arise out of nothing," she said. "Some kind of creature lived down there at some time."

I rubbed my arms, trying to hide the goosebumps that ran down them. The beast, whatever it was, did indeed still live down there. And at some point after we trespassed in its lair, it would hunt us.

EIGHT

I couldn't let them go down into the tunnels without knowing we wouldn't all make it out alive. They should have the chance to choose. I opened my mouth to tell them about my dream, but Istnofret spoke before I did.

"Are you going or not?" she asked.

I glanced back at the old woman. She still stood there, waiting.

"I think I should."

I could tell them when I got back.

Renni set down his packs with a sigh.

"Go on then," he said. "But be quick. We will wait here."

The old woman's face gave away nothing and a strange reluctance filled me as I approached. I didn't want to know what she wanted from me. Before I reached her, the woman disappeared into her cottage.

I hesitated at the door, peering in. The only illumination was what came through the doorway. Either there were no windows or the shutters were closed. A cottage of this size surely consisted of only one chamber. As I inhaled, my lungs filled with a smoke that made me dizzy almost straight away. Was she burning herbs? I muffled a cough and tried not to breathe too deeply. Hopefully, I wouldn't be here for long.

Light flared, burning my eyes, which had started to adjust to the darkness. The old woman sat cross-legged on the dirt floor. In front of her was a candle, which was the source of the sudden light, and a large bronze bowl filled with water. She gestured to the floor, indicating for me to sit opposite her. I sank down in front of her and copied her cross-legged pose. The heat from the candle was too warm in the smoky confines of the cottage.

The woman leaned over the bronze bowl, passing one hand through the air above it. Her eyes were closed as she murmured something that felt like a prayer, although it was in a language I didn't know. When she stared straight at me, I realised a milky film coated her eyes. Surely she could see nothing at all. Perhaps that was why there was so little light inside this cottage.

The woman gestured towards the bowl and I leaned over to peer in. It was perhaps two palms in height and four palms wide. Was I supposed to drink from it? I glanced up at her and she gestured again towards the bowl. How did she even know whether I looked at her or at it?

Eventually, the smokiness seemed to penetrate the water and it became cloudy. I waited for the woman to indicate I had stared into the bowl for long enough. Did she have nothing to say? Was this all she wanted from me?

A dark shape coalesced in the smoky water and my interest sharpened. Another few moments passed before I could make out what it was, and when I did, my blood felt like it froze in my veins.

It was a scarab. A night-black scarab burned into skin, bright blood dripping from its edges. The same image I had seen in my dreams. What did it mean?

The smoky water rippled and the scarab dissolved. I glanced up at the woman and she gestured towards the bowl again. Did she know what I had seen? I waited for a long time, but no other images appeared. My backside had gone numb and I badly needed to stretch my legs.

"I must return to my friends," I said.

"Ha." She gestured towards the bowl.

"There is nothing there." I tried to stem my rising frustration at wasting so much time. "I have seen nothing else."

She grunted and pointed to the bowl. With a sigh, I returned my gaze to the water.

I had no sense of how much time passed before the water stirred again. This time, the image was different. The first thing to appear was a woman's face. The water shifted around her and as it revealed more of her form, I saw she wore a ruffled gown in the style favoured by the Cretan women. She stood with her arms stretched out to either side. In each fist, she clasped a snake. One twitched, flicking its tail from side to side.

I gasped and drew back a little, suddenly afraid the woman might burst out of the water and thrust one of her snakes at me. The old woman reached across the bowl and grabbed my wrist, as if fearing I would leave and not see the rest of whatever it was she intended.

I tried to calm myself. It was just a picture in a bowl of water. It couldn't harm me. The woman's face seemed to shift and meld. Soon it was Meketaten who stared out at me, although she wore the woman's body and clutched her snakes. I held my breath, but the image didn't change again. The water rippled and the image dissolved.

The old woman released my wrist and made a shooing motion at me. It seemed I had seen what she wanted me to. When I reached the doorway, I stopped, wondering if she might speak now before I left, but she stared down at the bowl of water as if she could see it. Perhaps she had forgotten I was there.

NINE

When I emerged from the old woman's house, Behenu was perched on top of a crate. Istnofret lay on a blanket, staring up at the sky. Sabu and Tuta leaned against trees while Mahu sat with his back against one. Only Renni was still on his feet, pacing up and down. He came to meet me as I left the cottage.

"What did she want?" he asked.

"She had a bowl of water, which she wanted me to look at."

"You looked at a bowl of water? For three hours?"

"Three hours? Surely not."

Half an hour maybe. An hour at most.

"I wondered if I should go in after you," he said.

"I was perfectly safe. There was nobody there other than the woman."

We had reached the others by now.

"What did she say?" Istnofret turned her head so she could see me but didn't make any move to get up.

"She showed me a bowl of water," I said. "There were pictures in it."

"What kind of pictures?" Behenu's tone was sharp.

"A scarab," I said. "And a woman holding a pair of snakes. Have you heard of such a thing before?"

"I have heard of water being used to see images," she said. "Someone trained in such a thing can predict the future from what they see in the water."

"Surely not," I said.

Behenu shrugged, as if she didn't care whether I believed her.

"That is what I have heard," she said.

"But I have had no training in such a thing," I said. "Why was I able to see her pictures?"

"Perhaps she can make you see them. An intermediary, if you will."

"But what do they mean?"

"Did she not explain them to you?" Behenu asked.

"She didn't speak at all. Maybe I should have waited longer. Perhaps she might have if I had stayed long enough."

"Maybe you are not meant to understand them right now," Istnofret said. "They might be clues."

"Clues to what?" I asked.

"Perhaps even she doesn't know." Istnofret rose from her blanket and gave it a shake. "She might know only there was something you needed to see, but not what it means."

"This is all too mysterious," I said. "And far too elusive. How in the name of the goddess could she know any such thing?"

Istnofret folded the blanket and stashed it back in a pack.

"Given the things we have seen, I might have thought you would be more willing to accept what you do not understand," she said.

I frowned at her, not liking the feeling of being chastised.

"There is one more thing," I said. "The woman. At first she had a face I didn't know. But then she turned into Meketaten."

"The images have some meaning for you," Behenu said. "Even if you don't know what yet."

"We are wasting time standing here," Renni said before I could reply. "Did you see anything that made you think we should not go into the tunnels?"

Should I tell them I had seen the same scarab in a dream? The image made me uneasy, whereas the woman with the snakes gave me no sense of either good or bad. She simply was, even after she became Meketaten. Another image from my dreams rose in my mind, the one in which the beast hunted us through the tunnels. I pushed it down, having changed my mind about telling them. Renni hadn't asked about that. I wasn't lying by not telling them about that dream.

"No," I said. "I saw nothing that was obviously associated with the tunnels."

"Let's go, then," he said. "We have wasted far too much daylight."

We picked up our packs again and started across the grassy area in front of the ruins, leaving the old man to hopefully keep watch over the rest of our belongings.

"We approached from over there last time." Behenu pointed. "Remember we walked the length of one side and partway along another? Then I went across the rubble and found the place where the tunnel had caved in."

As we retraced our original path, I tried to avoid looking at the rubble. My earlier thought about the previous inhabitants being buried beneath them made me uneasy. Instead, I looked down at the lush grass, interspersed with patches of bright yellow flowers. Their scent mixed with a refreshing salty breeze from the ocean. With the sun beating down on me, I felt quite sleepy.

"Perhaps we could take a break," Istnofret suggested. Her words ended with an enormous yawn.

"I am feeling rather tired myself," Tuta said.

"I can hardly keep my eyes open," Behenu said. "Renni, can we stop for a while? A short rest before we enter the tunnels?"

Renni's own yawn interrupted his reply.

"It has been a long day," he said. "Maybe we could stop for a few minutes. Not long, though. I don't want to be entering the tunnels after sunset."

"We are almost there anyway." Istnofret dropped her packs. "A rest before we go down there will do us all good."

Mahu dropped to the grass and stretched out. He rested one arm over his eyes and seemed to be asleep even before I sat down.

"Just a few minutes," Renni said again.

"Should someone keep watch?" Sabu asked through a yawn.

Nobody replied. I closed my eyes and drifted off.

I woke some time later. My head was fuzzy and I struggled to open my eyes. The spell bottle at my chest burned against my skin. It must be that which woke me. A not-quite-heard echo lingered in my mind. *He is a trickster.* I sat up a little too quickly and my head spun. Sleep tugged at me and I wanted nothing more than to drift away again, but the spell bottle continued to burn. It had never been wrong when it warned me of danger. I finally noticed the sky was studded with stars.

"Renni?" My voice was croaky and I could hardly force out the words. "We have slept too long."

Renni stirred and mumbled something, but didn't wake.

"Istnofret, are you awake?" I asked.

She didn't reply.

"Behenu? Tuta?"

Still no response.

I tried to get up, but my limbs were heavy and it seemed like far too much effort. I should lie down and go back to sleep. After all, everyone else was.

Everyone else. There was nobody on guard.

"Sabu?" I called. "Mahu? Is anyone awake?"

Soft snores from Sabu were my only reply. I should go back to sleep and not worry about it. After all, look how peaceful they were. They all slept so soundly. There was no reason for me to be awake. I lay back down without even realising. I closed my eyes, but the spell bottle was a coal against my chest, keeping me awake. When I focused on the bottle, the pain sharpened my mind.

There was a spell at work here, I finally realised. Something — or someone — was making us sleep. Even now, I felt the magic tugging at my mind, urging me to sink back down into the soft, cool grass. I pressed the spell bottle against my skin so it hurt even more. The pain was the only thing keeping me awake. I went to Renni and shook his shoulder.

"Renni, wake up."

He murmured and rolled over, tucking his hands beneath his cheek.

"Renni, you have to get up. Something is wrong."

His deep breaths told me he was still sound asleep. I slid his dagger from the waistband of his *shendyt*.

"Renni, I am sorry about this."

I drew the dagger across his forearm, just a shallow cut, enough for blood to ooze out and to cause him some pain.

He was awake in an instant.

"By the gods, Samun, what are you doing?" He sat up and snatched the dagger from me. "Did you cut me?"

"It was the only way to wake you."

"What are you talking about?"

He finally noticed the night sky and the fact that everyone else still slept.

"How long did we sleep?" he asked.

"I don't know. I only woke up a few minutes ago and couldn't wake any of you."

He tucked the dagger back into his waistband and went to Tuta.

"Tuta, wake up, man."

He shook Tuta by the shoulders.

"Tuta." Renni shook him more firmly.

"You won't wake him like that," I said.

He went to Sabu, then Istnofret, shaking each of them. At length he pulled out his dagger and made a shallow cut in Tuta's arm, just as I had to him. Tuta woke and after a brief discussion, they woke everyone else in the same manner.

At last they were all on their feet, each with an oozing cut on their arm. I still clutched the spell bottle to my chest. My skin felt like it was on fire, but at least it kept me awake.

"What in the goddess's name happened?" Istnofret asked.

"I don't know," I said. "All I remember is that I was so sleepy."

"We all were," Behenu said. "I lay down and went straight to sleep."

"I think I started asking about guard duty, but fell asleep before I could finish." Sabu looked rather shame-faced. "I should have done better."

"No," Tuta said. "There was some strange magic at work here. It is nobody's fault we all fell asleep."

"Has anyone ever heard of such a thing?" Istnofret asked. "Behenu, you often have esoteric knowledge the rest of us don't. Do you know of anything like this?"

"I wish I knew something useful," Behenu said. "But I have never heard of such a thing outside of made-up tales."

"What tales?" Renni asked. "Tell us what you remember. It might be useful."

Behenu frowned a little as she thought.

"I don't remember the whole thing, but there was a tale I heard as a girl. Something about a woman who trespassed in a place of the gods and because they didn't want her there, they made her go to sleep."

"How long did she sleep?" Istnofret asked.

"I don't remember how the tale ended," Behenu said, "but I don't think she ever woke up."

We stared at each other. Their faces were pale and their eyes wide. I supposed I looked much the same. Was it possible that if my spell bottle hadn't woken me, we might have slept forever?

"I think we should move on." Renni's tone was grim. "And we need to be alert for anything strange. If you feel sleepy, tell us so we can keep you awake. But whatever you do, do not lie down. You might never wake up again."

TEN

As we resumed walking around the ruins, I felt solemn. We had almost failed to retrieve Intef and he wouldn't have even known we had tried. I checked myself for any desire to sleep, but whatever had affected us earlier seemed to have worn off. In fact, now that my head was clear, I felt refreshed. Energised. Invigorated.

"Perhaps we could go a little faster?" Tuta suggested.

"Yes, we are walking far too slowly." Istnofret already quickened her pace.

"I think I will run on ahead," Behenu said. "Have a look around, see if anything looks different."

"I will go with you," Tuta said.

They took off together.

"I am eager to see the tunnels you have all talked so much about," Sabu said. "I will catch up to them."

"Wait." Mahu grabbed him by the arm before he could run off. "Does this not seem strange to anyone else?"

"I was actually feeling the urge to run myself," Renni said.

"Me too," Istnofret said. "And you know I am not the type to want to run anywhere."

"I feel it too," Mahu said. "And that is why I know it is not natural.

My illness leaves me too weak and fatigued to ever want to run. So if I feel it, it must be another spell."

"But for what purpose?" I asked. "To make us run until we die from exhaustion?"

I didn't expect anyone to have an answer.

"What do we do about Behenu and Tuta?" Istnofret asked. "We won't be able to catch up to them now, even if we run."

"I think we should wait here," Renni said. "They will likely run all the way around the ruins and come up behind us. We only have to wait for them."

"And how do we convince them to stop?" she asked. "If this is another spell, they will probably run straight past us and keep going."

"We will tackle them," Sabu said. "Mahu and I can take Tuta. Renni, you take Behenu. She knows you better than she knows either of us. I am not sure how she will react if Mahu or I tackle her."

"Once they are on the ground, we can sit on them to hold them down," Istnofret said. "Samun and I can help with that."

"But how long do we hold them down?" I asked.

"Until they stop wanting to run," she said.

"I think we will know when it is over," Renni said. "In the meantime, perhaps we should stop and wait for them to come back around."

Before I could set down my packs, a sense of unease filled me. We shouldn't stop here. We should keep moving.

"I don't think I can stop," Istnofret said.

"Me either," Sabu said. "I have the strangest feeling that something bad will happen if I am not moving."

"So we keep walking but go as slowly as you can," Renni said. "The sleep spell wore off quickly enough once we were aware of it."

My legs still wanted to run, but I made myself walk slowly. It became increasingly painful. My muscles burned to move. My legs longed to stretch and flex and drive my body onwards. Just as I thought I couldn't keep myself from running any longer, footsteps pounded behind us.

"Here they come," Istnofret said, rather unnecessarily, for we had all turned to look.

"Get ready." Renni lined himself up in front of Behenu.

Sabu and Mahu moved into position.

As Behenu and Tuta approached, their faces were red and they gasped for breath. Behenu looked like she could barely hold herself up.

"Cannot stop," Tuta called as they approached. "Have to keep running."

"All is well," Renni called. "Just come to us."

Tuta darted around Sabu and Mahu, and nearly got past them. Sabu tackled him at the last moment, grabbing him around the waist, and they tumbled to the ground. Mahu flung himself on Tuta's arm. I ran to help.

"Sit on his back," Mahu said to me as he tried to keep hold of Tuta's arm.

Tuta writhed and struggled to get up. Sabu lay across his legs, his arms still around his waist. I sat on Tuta's back and he bucked me off. I tried again and managed to position myself on his upper back with my feet pressed against his loose arm. It felt like an age before Tuta stopped struggling. Finally, he lay still beneath us. By then, Sabu, Mahu and I panted almost as hard as he did.

Renni and Istnofret were still struggling with Behenu. Renni must have snatched her up as she ran past him, for he held her around the waist with her back against his chest. Istnofret had her arms around Behenu's knees. The girl still bucked and wriggled, trying to escape their grasp, but eventually she, too, grew still.

"Lie her down, Ist," Renni said, and they gently laid Behenu on the ground. "Keep hold of her, though."

"How much longer do we wait?" I asked.

Nobody answered, which was hardly a surprise. They knew no more than I did. Eventually, Tuta groaned.

"You can get off me," he said. "The compulsion has passed."

"How do we know that is true?" Sabu asked. "It could be a trick to make us let you up so you can keep running."

"It is no trick, I assure you," Tuta said. "I am exhausted anyway. I don't think I could run even if I wanted to."

We climbed off him and Tuta lay there for another few moments before he rolled over.

"I think I would have run until I dropped dead," he said. "Even as tired as I was, my legs only wanted to keep going. Faster and faster."

Behenu groaned in agreement.

"It is strange indeed," Renni said. "First the sleep spell, then the running spell. What next?"

"How will we even know if some other spell affects us?" Istnofret asked. "The urge to run seemed perfectly natural."

"We all have to be on guard against anything strange or different," Renni said.

"Perhaps we should say what we are feeling," I suggested. "We might detect the next spell faster."

"I hope there isn't a next one," Istnofret said.

"Are there not supposed to be twelve gates in the underworld?" Mahu asked. "Perhaps there are also twelve trials or tests or spells."

"But we aren't even in the underworld yet," I said. "We have to go through the tunnels."

"We don't know that for sure," Renni said. "We assumed that was the case last time because we emerged from the tunnel to find ourselves in a different place. But perhaps there is more than one way to get there, or perhaps we simply passed through some invisible barrier."

"But there are no gates here," I said. "And last time we knew we were somewhere else because it looked different from our world."

"I suppose that doesn't mean it always works like that," Tuta said. He sat up and coughed a little, but finally caught his breath.

"How will we understand anything if it works differently each time?" Istnofret sighed. "I thought I understood where we were going, but this is all different and now I don't know what to expect."

"We are together, Ist." Renni wrapped his arm around her shoulders. "It is confusing, yes, but as long as we stick together, we will figure it out."

"Might there be anything helpful in that scroll?" Tuta asked.

"The Book of Amduat?" I tried to remember where I had stowed it. "I think it might be in that smaller pack Behenu was carrying. Where are your packs, by the way?"

"We dropped them while we were running," Behenu said.

"I thought I might run faster if I wasn't weighed down." Tuta rubbed the back of his head, a sheepish look on his face. "I am sorry. I can go on ahead and find them."

"We should stick together," Renni said. "If you go ahead, you might feel you need to hurry and then you might want to run again. And it will be harder to tackle you a second time now you know what to expect."

"I am truly sorry," Tuta said. "I feel like I let you all down."

"These are strange magics," Sabu said. "I don't think anyone could be prepared for such a thing. I know I wasn't."

"I am not sure I believed we were going to the underworld until just now," Mahu said.

"It is a difficult thing to understand," Renni said. "I would not believe it if I hadn't seen it myself. Now, Behenu and Tuta, can you both walk?"

"I think so." Behenu started to get up but toppled over.

"Whoah, steady there." Renni grabbed her hands and hauled her to her feet. "Just stand there for a moment while your legs adjust. You must be exhausted."

"I have never run so far or so fast in my life," Behenu said.

"I don't know how you kept up with me." Tuta cast her an admiring look as he got to his feet, no less unsteady than she. "As guards, we are used to training hard, and I have spent countless hours running. But that was difficult even for me."

Behenu shrugged. "It wasn't so bad at first, but then I got really tired. I couldn't have kept running if it wasn't for the spell."

"Can you walk?" Renni asked.

She took a few tentative steps.

"My legs are shaking, but I think I can go slowly," she said.

"Let's move on," Renni said. "Stay alert, everyone. We have no idea what might be next."

ELEVEN

W e finally reached the place where Behenu and Tuta had dropped their packs.

"Should we rest for a while?" Istnofret asked. "Behenu doesn't look like she can walk much further."

"I can keep going," Behenu said. "And I am so tired that I fear falling asleep if we stop."

"We don't know whether the sleeping spell is finished," Renni said. "I don't think we can risk sitting down."

"Perhaps we should check the Book of Amduat now?" Sabu asked. "As long as we are standing, it will be hard to fall asleep."

"There is nothing in the Book about anything like what we have experienced tonight," I said. "I have been thinking about it since Tuta asked. It is all about the various gods and goddesses that guard the gates and about the things we might see on the way. There is nothing about sleeping spells or running spells, or at least not in the version we have."

"It must be the middle of the night by now," Tuta said. "We need to decide what to do. Do we find somewhere to camp until morning, or do we keep going and try to reach the tunnels?"

"Perhaps we should go back?" Sabu suggested. "Find somewhere to spend the rest of the night, well away from the ruins. A safe place, a good sleep. We can try again tomorrow and be better prepared now we know what we will face."

"But what if the spells are specific to the locations where we encountered them?" Istnofret asked. "If we go back, we might hit them again."

"Perhaps we would come across them the other way around this time," Tuta said. "The running spell first, then the sleeping spell."

"We don't know," Renni said, "and we cannot afford to risk it. I think the only thing we can do is keep going. When we find the place where we entered the tunnels last time, we will decide what to do next."

Nobody voiced any disagreement, so we set off again. As we walked, my stomach growled, reminding me I hadn't eaten since breakfast. We had plenty of supplies and I was about to suggest we eat while we walked when the most delicious aroma reached my nostrils.

"Do you smell that?" I asked.

"It is probably me," Tuta said. "I am very sweaty after all that running."

"Ugh, me too," Behenu said. "I need a bath."

"No, just smell it. It is…" I sniffed the air again. "Melon juice."

"I cannot smell melon juice, but I do smell roasting meat," Sabu said.

"Oh yes," Tuta said. "Definitely roasting meat. Pig, I think. Maybe a hen as well."

"Fresh bread," Behenu said with a groan. "Someone is baking bread and it smells wonderful."

I inhaled deeply, but couldn't smell either roasting meats or baking bread.

"No, it is melon juice," I said. "I don't know how you could mistake it for anything else."

"It is indeed a fruity smell, but not melon juice," Istnofret said. "It smells more like figs to me. Figs that have ripened in the sunshine and are fit to bursting."

"Duck roasting over a campfire," Renni said. "I have smelled that enough times to recognise it anywhere."

"I smell nothing but cheese," Mahu said. "A delicate goat cheese, if I am not mistaken."

"Someone nearby is preparing a feast," Behenu said.

My stomach growled again, louder this time.

"Perhaps whoever it is might share their feast with us?" Istnofret said. "After all, they obviously have an abundance of food."

"It is that way, I think." I pointed in the direction the melon juice aroma seemed to come from.

"Let's go," Tuta said. "My mouth is salivating at the thought of that roasting pig."

"Wait," Renni said. "Can you not see what is happening?"

My stomach growled so loudly I almost couldn't hear Renni over it.

"Come on," Istnofret said with a moan. "I am so hungry, and those ripe figs are all I can think about now."

"We have plenty of supplies in our packs." Renni opened one and retrieved a loaf of bread. "Here, Behenu, divide this up and I'll find some dried meat to go with it."

Behenu waved him away.

"I am not eating day-old bread carried around in a stinking pack when I can smell bread being freshly baked right now."

"Behenu, there is no baking bread," Renni said. "It is another spell."

Istnofret sniffed the air again.

"That is no magic, Renni, just ripe figs," she said. "You can stay here and eat your old bread if you want, but I am going to find those figs."

She walked away, but Renni dropped the bread and grabbed her arm.

"Ist, listen to me. We all smell different things. You smell figs, Behenu smells bread, I smell roasting duck. Do you smell any bread or meat?"

"Of course not," she said crossly. "I can smell nothing but figs and right now, the only thing standing between me and those figs is you."

"It is not real, Ist," Renni said. "I cannot smell your figs at all. I don't smell Behenu's bread or Samun's melon juice or Tuta's roasting pig. All I can smell is duck being cooked over a campfire. Does that not seem strange to you? The way none of us can smell anything other than our own very favourite food?"

Of course, Renni was right. As soon as I realised, the aroma disappeared. I inhaled deeply, but I definitely couldn't smell melon juice anymore.

"It is gone," I said, a little mournfully. "Once you realise it is just another spell, it goes away."

"It is true," Behenu said. "I cannot smell baking bread anymore."

The others murmured agreement, all sounding as disappointed as she. Only Istnofret shook her head and refused to listen.

"I know what I can smell." She tried to pull her arm out of Renni's grip. "Let go of me. I want to find those figs."

"The figs don't exist, Ist," I said. "They are not real."

"Of course they are real." She gave me a withering glare. "I can smell them. Are you saying I am imagining it?"

"You are not imagining it. It is a spell." Renni still held fast to her arm. "Accept it, Ist. We cannot move on until we all recognise the spell."

"You are being ridiculous," she said. "All of you. Now let me go. I will come back once I have found the figs and you will all be sorry you were so mean to me."

"What are we going to do if she won't listen?" I asked.

"I cannot hold her and carry all my packs," Renni said.

"We have plenty of rope," Sabu said. "We can tie her to you, Renni."

"You will not tie me up like an animal." Istnofret's voice was indignant and her face went bright red.

I had never seen her so angry.

"Ist, it is just until the spell fades," I said.

She glared at me.

"I suppose this amuses you? Takes you back to being queen or pharaoh or whatever you call yourself these days."

Her words stung, as I was sure she intended.

"I don't call myself anything these days," I said, a little sadly. "And I have apologised over and over for the things I did."

"You had better watch out." Istnofret glared around at the others. "She will find reasons to tie you all up soon enough. We will all be under threat of execution if we don't do what she says."

"To what end, Ist?" I asked. "You are the only one still succumbing to the spell. You are the only one who can still smell your favourite food."

"I know what I can smell," she said. "And I am going to find those figs."

"You are not being rational, Ist." Renni's tone was far more patient than she deserved.

"Let go of me," she yelled, redoubling her efforts to twist herself from his grasp.

Renni held on, his face grim.

What would happen if she got away from him? Would she keep walking, endlessly searching for the figs but never able to find them? Would she refuse to eat anything else and eventually starve to death for want of the magical figs? I tried to help by grabbing Istnofret's other arm, but she shoved me away and I fell. Sabu managed to get hold of her free hand, while Tuta hauled me to my feet.

"Are you hurt?" he asked.

I held up my palms to show him the grazes on them.

"I am well enough," I said.

"Maybe we should keep walking," Behenu suggested. "The other magics wore off once we moved on. Perhaps this one will do the same."

"Let's go then," Renni said. "I am afraid the rest of you will need to manage Sabu's and my packs."

We divided their packs between us and kept walking, although more slowly now. My load was too heavy and I wouldn't be able to carry it for long. Renni and Sabu dragged Istnofret between them, still writhing and yelling. I tried to block out the noise. It was awful to see her like this and I hated that she had to be restrained, but it was for her own safety. Eventually, Istnofret quietened and soon she walked calmly between Renni and Sabu. She sniffled a little.

"Ist?" Renni asked. He still held fast to her arm, obviously not yet trusting the spell had passed.

"I am sorry," she said with a sob. "I acted appallingly."

Renni pulled her against his chest and wrapped his arms around her.

"You were spelled," he said. "We all were."

"But why did everyone else come to their senses so much sooner than me? What is wrong with me that I kept wanting to go after those gods-damned figs?"

"Well, you do really like figs," Renni said with a chuckle as he wiped the tears from her cheeks.

Istnofret laughed too, although it ended in a sob. She buried her face in Renni's chest for a few moments, then pulled away.

"Let's keep moving," she said.

"I think we should tie ourselves together," Renni said. "We brought plenty of string. We could tie one wrist of each of us. Then, if anyone succumbs to another spell, they won't be able to run off on their own."

We all agreed it was a sound plan and in just a few minutes, we were tied together in a row by our left wrists.

I felt more hopeful as we set off again. At least now we weren't at risk of losing anyone.

TWELVE

The moon was high in the sky by now, just a half orb, but still sufficient to light our way. My sandals sank into soft grass and the cool night air echoed with the chirps of insects and the hoot of an owl. I kept checking for any unusual aromas but smelled nothing other than grass and flowers. The more peaceful our surroundings seemed, the more anxious I became. What other spell lurked in wait for us? At length, we reached the place where Behenu had climbed across the ruins to the hole that led down into the tunnels.

"Perhaps we should keep going," Sabu said, as we stared across the ruins. "There doesn't seem to be much point in sitting here waiting for another spell to find us."

"Should I go see if the path across is still as stable as it was last time?" Behenu asked.

Renni frowned as he studied the ruins.

"I don't think anyone should go over there unless we intend to continue. What if there is some spell that draws you on, either down into the tunnels or across the ruins? We would have to come after you, and that will be more dangerous in the dark."

"I think we should wait until morning," Tuta said. "I am still tired from running and Behenu must be too. It would be better if we are all rested before we go any further."

I nodded my agreement, even as I tried not to think about the beast that lurked down there, waiting to hunt us. Sabu was the only one who thought we should keep going, but he conceded defeat and we set about making ourselves comfortable. We agreed we should remain tied together while we rested, although we divided into two groups — men and women — tied to separate lengths of string to allow us to go off and relieve ourselves with some modicum of privacy.

We didn't bother with a fire since we had brought no supplies that needed to be cooked. Instead, we ate chunks of bread with cheese and strips of dried pig.

"It is not quite as good as the roasting pig I smelled earlier," Tuta said a little ruefully as he chewed his dried meat.

"Nor is the bread," Behenu said. "It is already going stale."

"I think I dropped the bread I got out earlier," Renni said.

"It doesn't matter," Behenu said. "We have plenty of supplies."

"And more with the rest of our packs," Sabu said.

"I wonder if the old man is still watching them?" Tuta asked. "When we didn't return by sunset, he might have gone home."

"Nothing we can do about it now." Renni lay back on his blanket and made himself comfortable. "He will either be there when we return or he won't. Let's just get some rest. Tomorrow will probably be a long day."

"I will take first watch," Sabu said.

"I will go next," Mahu said. "Wake me in a couple of hours."

I finished my meal and lay down with a blanket wrapped around me. I shivered a little and wished we had built a fire after all. It was at times like this that I particularly missed Intef. The breeze was chill and the heat from his body beside me would have been welcome tonight.

"I am coming, Intef," I whispered as I pulled the blanket more tightly around me. "Tomorrow, I hope. Just hold on a little longer."

For once, my sleep was devoid of dreams and I was the first to wake. The sun was only just peeking over the horizon, and around me the others still breathed deeply except for Tuta, who sat with a blanket draped around his shoulders. He must have been the last to have guard duty overnight. I should offer to take a turn tonight.

The others stirred and soon I was occupied with breakfast and packing everything away. In reasonably short order, there was nothing left to do but make our way across the ruins.

"Behenu, you go first again, since you are still the lightest," Renni said. "We will tie you to a long piece of string in case you encounter any more strange spells. It might not be strong enough if we need to stop you from running off, but we don't have any rope that long, so it will have to do. Go carefully and don't trust that what was stable last time still is."

"I will be careful," Behenu said.

She waited while Renni fished out the skein of string and tied one end around her left wrist with the other around his. He then released her from the string tying us women together.

"Ready?" he asked.

She nodded.

"Oh, be careful," Istnofret said.

"You be careful," Behenu retorted. "And don't go off looking for magic figs."

As I watched her make her way across the rubble, I remembered how it felt to clamber over while wondering whether the tunnel underneath might collapse at any moment. Even knowing we had successfully traversed the ruins before didn't make it less nerve-wracking this time.

"Samun, are you well?"

I hadn't noticed Istnofret beside me until she spoke.

"I am fine," I said.

"You were rubbing your belly just now as you watched Behenu."

"Was I?"

I hadn't noticed, but it made sense considering I was picturing myself heavily pregnant and unsteady on my feet as I made my way across the rubble. Even though most of the others had safely crossed, I had feared my heavier weight would be too much for the ruins to bear. Intef had been behind me every step of the way.

"We might see Intef today," she said. "How do you feel about that?"

"I don't know, to be honest. I am afraid he might still hate me and I don't know how we will convince Keeper to release him. We might have come all this way and still have to leave him there."

"We will find a way." Her tone was nothing but confident. "Between us all, we will figure out how to get him back. You know Renni won't leave him there. Not after coming all this way to get him."

This was probably a good time to tell her how I intended to offer myself in exchange for Intef. I held my tongue, though. She would try to talk me out of it. They all would, and it would be a waste of energy. We needed to focus on the tunnels. We had bigger things to worry about right now than whether I should stay in Intef's place. Behenu's shout interrupted my morose thoughts. She had reached the place where the tunnel had collapsed.

"It is still accessible," she called. "The hole looks a little bigger, but the rocks we climbed down are still there."

"Stay there," Renni called. "We will come to you."

Since Behenu had encountered no spells on the way over, Renni untied the strings holding us together.

"Remember, we must stay on the path Behenu took," he said. "We know that part is stable, but other areas might collapse at any time. I will go first. Watch where I walk and try to take exactly the same path. Samun and Istnofret, you come after me. You men, wait until they are across before you follow. Is everyone ready?"

I nodded and hitched my packs a little higher over my shoulders. My heart pounded uncomfortably hard and my legs trembled a little. There was no reason to be so nervous. We had made this journey twice already and we just saw Behenu cross safely.

Istnofret and I made our way across the ruins, and then it was Tuta's turn. He was halfway to us when there came a rumble of rubble and a cloud of dust. When the dust cleared, Tuta was gone.

"Tuta!" Renni called. "Are you well?"

There was no reply.

"He fell down into the tunnels," Sabu called back.

He had already started across and was midway between the safety of the grass and the place where Tuta disappeared.

"He has fallen, yes, but we don't know where he landed," Renni said.

"There is at least one section of the tunnel that is in a different place," I said. "It is neither our world nor the underworld, but somewhere else."

My shadow led us through there last time. The memory reminded me of my promise, but there was no time to talk to it now.

"You mean he has gone straight into the underworld?" Sabu asked.

I shrugged. We had no way of knowing where he might be.

Sabu approached the place where Tuta disappeared and leaned down to peer into the hole.

"Tuta, can you hear me?" he called.

"Careful," Renni said. "Tuta crashing through like that might have weakened more of the surrounding area. Come over here and we will decide what to do."

Sabu backed up and made a wide detour around where Tuta disappeared. It meant he had to leave the path we had established as safe, but he reached us without incident. Mahu was the last to cross over and he followed Sabu's path.

"We cannot leave him," Mahu said as he reached us.

"Tuta, can you hear us?" Istnofret called.

"What if he is injured?" Behenu asked, wringing her hands. She looked rather pale. Perhaps she cared more for Tuta than she had let on. "The fall might have knocked him unconscious. He could be lying down there and unable to respond."

Renni's face showed his conflicted feelings.

"Let's think this through," he said. "Tuta has either gone to some other place, in which case searching for him is futile, or he has fallen through to the tunnels and is injured."

"Even if he has gone somewhere else, can we not follow him?" Sabu asked. "If we jump down in the place where he fell, surely we would be wherever he is."

"We don't know it works like that," I said. "You might end up in a different place, or you might find yourself in the tunnels and with no sign of Tuta."

Sabu shook his head.

"I don't understand any of this," he said.

"Neither do we, man," Renni said. "But we have seen enough to know this place is unpredictable. If the gods don't want us to find Tuta, they will shield him from us. If he is injured, we cannot carry him, so we may as well leave him there for now. We will look for him when we return."

"If he is badly injured, he may not last until tonight," Behenu said.

Renni sighed.

"What do you suggest, then?" he asked. "I am reluctant to send anyone after him in case we end up with a second person missing. We won't even know if they are in the same place as Tuta. Our mission is to retrieve Intef. Would you have us diverted for the sake of one man who might already be dead or might be off wandering the underworld, never to be found by us?"

Behenu dropped her gaze and shook her head.

"We need to find Intef," she said.

"So let's do that," Renni said. "We will keep our eyes and ears open for any sign of Tuta. Perhaps he has indeed fallen down into the tunnels, in which case we might find him. If he is in the underworld, we may encounter him there."

"Shouldn't we at least search the surrounding tunnels?" Mahu asked. "The place where he fell is not that far from us."

"It is not possible to go straight there," Renni said. "The tunnels are a labyrinth of twists and turns, and they are dark as night. It is next to impossible to maintain any sense of direction."

"But we will see the hole in the ceiling," Sabu said. "I don't understand why you think it will be so hard to find him. We have only to check a few turns, look for the light, then see if he is there."

"You will see for yourself when we get down there," Renni said. "The tunnels are unpredictable, and they are not entirely of this world."

Even if Tuta had fallen down into the tunnels, the beast might find him before we did. Tuta might be nothing but a pile of gnawed bones before we found him. I had known that not all of us would make it out of the tunnels alive, but I hadn't considered the possibility that more than one might lose their life.

THIRTEEN

We made our way down the staircase of boulders and gathered in the tunnel.

"Right then," Renni said. "Sabu, we need lamps. Mahu, string and charcoal."

As they prepared themselves, the back of my neck tingled. Anything might creep up behind me in the darkness. I moved to stand with my back against the wall.

"Samun?" Istnofret sidled up to me.

"I don't know where my dagger is." Why was it never where it was supposed to be? I fumbled for the pouch that should have been at my waist. "Where is my pouch?"

"In one of the packs, probably." Istnofret shrugged, seemingly unconcerned. "The men will have their daggers and if anything happens, we will only be in the way."

"I need my dagger." I set down my packs and rummaged through them. "Where is it?"

"Samun, what is wrong?" Istnofret put her hand on my shoulder, but I shook her off. "You are acting strangely."

"I just want my dagger. Is that too much to ask?"

"Why? You have never cared about where your dagger is before. Think of all the times Intef chastised you for not having it on you. What has changed? Why are you so scared?"

I inhaled shakily. I should tell them what I knew. They should have the chance to decide whether to continue with the knowledge that one of us would die. But nobody would come with me if I told them. They all knew it would be dangerous when they agreed to come, so what did it matter if they didn't know about my dream? They had already committed to our mission, as Renni called it. I steeled myself. I wouldn't jeopardise the mission. We had to get Intef out of that place.

"I just don't like it down here." I rummaged through various packs and tried to tell myself I might have been mistaken that my dream about the beast was a true dream. "You know tunnels make me nervous. I would feel better if I knew where my dagger was."

Istnofret studied me and I thought she would press me for a better answer, but at length she sighed and helped me search.

"Here it is." She pulled my pouch out of a pack. "It was wrapped in your blanket."

"Thank you." I looped the pouch around my waist. "I should be more careful about keeping it on me."

"What aren't you saying, Samun? Have you dreamed about the tunnels?"

"Of course not. I would have told you, wouldn't I?"

"No, I don't think you would."

"Everyone ready to go?" Renni asked before I could think of a reply.

Everyone murmured agreement, except Istnofret and I. Renni shot us a quizzical look.

"Ready," Istnofret said.

I only nodded, not trusting myself to speak. I was too close to blurting out what I hadn't told them.

"Let's go then," Renni said. "We will tie ourselves together again. I'll go first with Istnofret and Behenu behind me, then Sabu and Samun. Mahu, you'll be in the rear to keep watch behind us. If we encounter danger, Sabu, your task is to keep Samun safe. I will look after Ist and Behenu."

We assembled ourselves in the order he indicated and Renni tied our wrists to a long piece of string. He passed Sabu some charcoal.

"I'll mark our path along the tunnel wall. Sabu, you mark it on the floor. That will give us two chances to find our way back."

"Got it." Sabu took the charcoal from him.

"Should I mark our way as well?" Mahu asked.

"No, you keep watch behind us," Renni said. "Sabu, in the middle as he is, can better afford to be distracted than you can."

We set off, and I noticed both Istnofret and Behenu had their daggers in their hands. I fumbled in my pouch. I would not be the only one without mine ready. Not this time.

Renni followed the same pattern we used previously, taking the left turn each time the tunnel branched. We hadn't been walking for long before the tunnel ahead grew brighter.

"Light up ahead," Renni said. "Go carefully. If this is where Tuta fell, it might still be unstable."

But although there was indeed a hole in the tunnel roof, I saw nothing other than dust and fallen rubble.

"Someone has been here recently." Sabu pointed. "Fresh footprints in the dust."

"And a piece of rope." Behenu pointed to a neatly coiled rope which seemed to have been forgotten.

I looked around, hoping I too might spot a clue. Perhaps even something that would lead us to Tuta. But as I studied the fallen rubble and the boulders that seemed to provide a staircase up to the surface, the place felt familiar.

"Wait a minute," Renni said. "I think we are back where we started."

"It is because we kept turning left," Sabu said. "That is bound to lead us back to the beginning sooner or later."

"That is what we did last time and we didn't go back to the same place," Behenu said.

"Somebody controls these tunnels and we will go only where they want us to." Istnofret gave me a hard look. "I don't suppose you know anything about that?"

"Me? I'm not doing it."

She narrowed her eyes at me but said nothing further.

"Let's try again," Renni said. "Perhaps we missed a turn at some point, and that led us back here."

Renni was unlikely to make that kind of mistake, and it was even more unlikely that none of us noticed if he did. But there was nothing else to do but try again. We set off along the tunnel, once again taking every left turn.

Once again, we ended up back where we started.

"That was not the path we took last time," Sabu said. "I never saw any of my chalk marks."

"Neither did I." Renni sighed and scratched his head. "And yet here we are."

"So what now?" Istnofret asked. "There is no point spending the day going around and around."

"What other choice do we have?" he asked. "If it is true that someone controls the tunnels, we can only go where they want us to. Perhaps we need to make a certain number of passes before they will let us move on."

"Like a spell?" Behenu asked. "One that you would say a certain number of times before it becomes effective?"

"What do you know of such spells?" I asked her.

Behenu's face became shuttered, and I regretted my question. She never reacted well when I asked anything about her previous life.

"Sorry," I muttered.

She shook her head and turned away.

"Our choices are to keep trying or to give up," Renni said. "I don't know about the rest of you, but I am not ready to give up yet."

"Let's keep going then," I said.

Round and round we went. Five times. Six. Seven.

"This is ridiculous," Istnofret said as we stopped to rest at the place where we started. "We cannot just keep going around."

"Do you have another suggestion?" Renni asked. "Tell me then, because I cannot think of anything else."

Be careful of the jackal. He is a trickster. The words echoed in my memory. Where had I heard them?

"What if one of the gods controls the tunnels?" I asked. "Anubis maybe. It is his gates we are trying to reach after all."

"Are you suggesting he might try to stop us from getting there?" Renni asked.

He is a trickster.

"Not stop us," I said. "Delay us maybe. Or teach us a lesson on the way."

"But what kind of lesson could we learn down here?" Istnofret asked.

Nobody responded. Likely everyone did the same as me: hope someone else might think of a lesson we could learn from navigating these endless tunnels.

"Trust," Behenu said eventually. "Maybe we are supposed to learn to trust that whoever controls the tunnels will lead us to the right place."

"Are you suggesting we stop marking our turns?" Renni asked. "We would quickly become lost."

"Perhaps that is the point," I said. "How better can we show we trust Anubis, if that is who controls the tunnels, than to give up marking our path?"

"Should we also take random turns?" Istnofret asked.

"Yes," I said. "By always turning left, we are trying to control our passage."

"I don't like this, Samun," Renni said. "I really don't. Failure could mean our lives. Are you willing to risk that?"

"It is not up to me," I said. "Let everyone decide for themselves. If anyone doesn't want to take the risk, let them leave now. They can go back up top and wait for us there."

At least I had given them the chance to stay behind. I tried to pretend I believed this was as good as telling them what I knew.

"I think we have to risk it," Istnofret said. "Either that or we climb back up out of here and give up."

"I am not giving up on Intef," I said. "Even if you all decide to leave, I will keep going."

"I will come with you," Sabu said. "Although I don't like it, I think you might be correct that we need to show trust."

"Mahu?" Renni asked. "Behenu?"

"I agree," Behenu said.

We waited for Mahu's reply. His face was conflicted, but he sighed and nodded.

"I will come too," he said.

I turned back to Renni.

"Well, then?" I asked.

He sighed.

FOURTEEN

We set off again, this time turning at random and without marking our path. I could tell from the set of Renni's shoulders that he still wasn't happy, but I was certain this was what we were meant to do. If Anubis was indeed a trickster, we needed to play his game.

We walked for a long time, but didn't return to where we had started. I tried not to study the tunnel walls for signs they were about to collapse. As Renni told me when we were in the tunnels in Hattusa, this place had stood for a long time. It was unlikely to fall down while we were inside. Eventually Renni stopped.

"We may as well take a break," he said. "Rest and have something to eat. We might be down here for some time yet."

"Should we go back?" Istnofret asked. "We have walked for hours. Surely it is night by now."

"Well past sunset, I would judge," Renni said. "No point going all the way back, even if we could find our way. We would just have to do it again tomorrow. I suggest we rest for a while, then keep going."

Nobody disagreed, although from the look on Mahu's face, Istnofret wasn't the only one who wanted to go back. We ate bread and more strips of dried pig. I wrapped a blanket around my shoulders and leaned against the tunnel wall, hoping to sleep for a while.

"You may as well lie down," Renni said to me. "We will stop here for a few hours."

"I am fine like this."

I couldn't tell him I feared not being able to get up quickly enough when the beast found us. With my head resting against the rocky wall, I closed my eyes but kept one hand on my pouch. As tired as I was from walking all day, I couldn't sleep. Not when every time I closed my eyes, I saw myself running through the tunnels, the beast's breath hot on my neck. If it caught me, I would never make it to Intef. The others might find him, but I would never see him again.

I must have fallen asleep, because eventually I dreamed.

At first the dream was like those I had experienced lately — a series of seemingly unconnected images. The row of baboons. The scarab that dripped blood. *Be careful of the jackal. He is a trickster.* Something reaching for me. It wanted something from me. Or it wanted me. A girl, not the one I had seen with Intef in previous dreams, although this one was around the same age. Time seemed to pass and I saw the girl again when she was older. She was the woman from the bowl of water. She stared at me with eyes that seemed to see a different world.

When I woke, I could make no sense of the dreams. There was no true dream hidden amongst them as far as I could tell — I had not seen any alternative endings — but that didn't mean they didn't still hold truth. The snake woman was the one that bothered me the most. I had seen her three times now. I supposed that meant I would encounter her at some stage, but whether she would be ally or foe, I had no idea.

By the next day, Mahu's face was pale and walking seemed to exhaust him. He had looked like this on the ship from Rhakotis. I figured this must be one of the bad days he mentioned, where he would stay in bed. Since we were all tied together, he had no choice but to keep up, but by the time we next stopped to rest, he swayed on his feet.

"Sit down, man," Renni said to him. "We will rest here for a while."

"I don't think I will be able to get up again if I do," Mahu said. "Better that I stay on my feet while I can."

He put down his packs, though. When we set off again, Mahu reached for them, but Renni stopped him.

"We will divide them between the rest of us," he said.

"I can manage," Mahu said, rather faintly.

"I don't think you can," Renni said. "Better that you use your strength to keep walking. Between all of us, we can carry your packs."

He divided Mahu's packs between us, giving me one of the smaller ones. The extra weight was noticeable, but it wasn't more than I could cope with.

The next couple of days were much the same. After walking until we were tired, we stopped to eat and rest. We took turns to keep watch while the others slept, except for Mahu, who walked in a daze and slept so heavily that Renni decided it was best if he didn't keep watch. We neither saw nor heard any sign of even so much as a rat living in the tunnels, but instead of assuaging my fears, I became increasingly afraid. Every time we turned a corner, I expected to see the beast ahead of us. When Mahu's sandal scuffed against the rocks, I feared he would be gone, taken by the beast without us even noticing. Renni came to sit beside me when we stopped to rest.

"You need to calm yourself, Samun," he said. "Everyone else is picking up on your fear and it is making them uneasy."

"I didn't realise it was so obvious," I muttered, a little embarrassed.

"Want to tell me what you are so worried about? Maybe I can help."

I shook my head.

"It is nothing," I said. "I am being silly. You know tunnels make me uneasy."

He studied me while I looked down at my hands and pretended not to notice.

"I know you well enough to know it is unlikely to be nothing," he said. "And I think it is more than just your fear of being underground. But I also know that if you are not ready to tell anyone, I won't be able to coax it out of you. So I won't ask again, but please try to appear calm, even if you don't feel it."

He went to sit with Istnofret for a while. My eyes burned. I had been so absorbed in my fear that I hadn't realised the impact it was having on everyone else. I jumped a little as Behenu sat beside me, but she didn't speak. When I snuck a glance at her, she wasn't even looking at me.

"Have you, too, come to tell me I am making everyone afraid?" I didn't mean to sound bitter, but it came out that way, anyway.

"No, I just..." Her voice trailed off, and she sighed. "I am worried about Tuta. Do you think he is well?"

I hesitated, not knowing how to reply. I knew no more about Tuta's fate than she did. When I didn't respond, Behenu sighed again.

"Samun, do you want to know why I never talk about Syria or my childhood?"

I nodded, hardly daring to breathe.

"It is because there were so many expectations on me. I was expected to be a certain kind of person. To live a certain kind of life. To do certain kinds of things. Nobody ever asked what *I* wanted. They always assumed I wanted to be the person they all wanted me to be."

"And you didn't?"

She leaned back against the rocks and stared up at the ceiling for a while.

"I don't really know. When Horemheb took me, I was very young. I wasn't old enough to decide whether what I wanted was the same as what my father wanted. Maybe I was not even old enough to realise there might be a difference. I knew, though, that I didn't have a choice. In a way, it was almost a relief to be taken away from all that. To a place where nobody knew me and there were no expectations about who I had to be."

"But you were a slave. Surely what your father wanted of you, whatever it was, would be better than being a slave."

"Better." She gave a heavy sigh. "Better for who?"

Before I could figure out how to reply, Renni said our break was over. We walked for another two days with no sign of either Tuta or any way out of the tunnels.

"We are almost out of supplies," Behenu said as we stopped to rest. "There is enough for another meal or two, but no more."

"So we ration what we have left," Renni said.

He came to look over her shoulder as she rummaged through the supplies.

"We can eat half of what we have been," he said.

"And what do we do once we have eaten it all?" Istnofret asked. "These tunnels seem to go forever and we might well wander in here for the rest of our lives without finding a way out."

"What do you suggest then?" he asked. "We agreed we need to allow Anubis, or whoever controls this place, to lead us where he wants. We have little hope of finding our way back, even at half rations. It seems to me all we can do is trust there is some purpose to this and keep going."

He looked at each of us, but nobody voiced any disagreement.

"Please," he said. "If you can think of something else, say it. I don't fancy the idea of starving down here."

"I think we need to keep going," Sabu said. "All we can do is hope that whoever controls the tunnels will allow us to get to wherever they are leading us."

Nobody voiced any disagreement, so we rested a while longer, then picked up our packs and moved on. We had only been walking for a few minutes when the darkness lightened.

"I think there's a break in the roof," Renni said. "There's light ahead."

Encouraged, we walked faster. Around the next turn, we found a place where the roof had collapsed.

"Thank Isis," Istnofret said with a heavy sigh.

"I suppose the question is, do we go up or do we keep walking?" Renni said.

"What? Of course we go up," Istnofret said. "Why would we keep going?"

Renni shrugged. "Maybe whoever controls these tunnels is testing us. Seeing if we will take the easy way out."

"Even so, we are almost out of supplies," she said. "We have no choice but to see what is up there. If it is our world, we can get more supplies and come back. But maybe it is not our world. Maybe we have finally reached the underworld."

"Let's go," Sabu said. "Even if it is still our world, I could do with a break from the tunnels and the darkness."

"I would kill for the chance to sleep on something that is not rock," Mahu said.

"And a bath," Behenu added.

They all looked at me.

"Samun?" Renni asked. "Do you agree?"

I nodded, although I felt a little cowardly. Despite the days of walking, the journey seemed too easy. If I had learned anything about the gods by now, it was that they didn't let us achieve anything easily.

"Let's go up," I said.

FIFTEEN

W e climbed up the boulders — strange how there was always a pile of rocks conveniently positioned just so to allow us to climb up or down — and emerged outside. Renni and Sabu had to help Mahu up, as he didn't have the strength to do it alone.

The sunlight burnt my eyes and at first all I could do was close them against its brightness. Even that was too much, hot red against my eyelids. I couldn't stand with my eyes closed all day, though, so I pried them open. Tears ran down my cheeks as my eyes adjusted.

When I could see somewhat, I realised the sun wasn't even that bright, although it was directly overhead. It was that strange, muted light we had previously experienced in the underworld, like late afternoon just before the sun started to set.

"I think we have reached the underworld," Istnofret said.

"I was hoping we might find Tuta when we got out of the tunnels," Behenu said.

We could all see he wasn't here. Last time we emerged near the Gates of Anubis, which were guarded by Keeper of the Lake. That was where Intef was. Now we stood in the middle of a plainlands, covered with knee-high grasses and small shrubs, much like the landscape of Babylonia. There were no palace ruins, nor the Gates of Anubis, nor anything else. No hills, no trees, no houses. Just plainlands as far as I could see. My heart sank. This was not where we left Intef.

"In the middle of nowhere," Istnofret said glumly. "Nowhere to get supplies."

"Where are the gates?" Sabu asked.

"Not here," she said. "This is a different place."

"What do we do now?" he asked. "I assume we don't know how to find the gates from here?"

"I suppose we keep walking," Renni said. "But which way?"

I studied the landscape, looking for some clue. Was the light different in that direction?

"That way." I pointed. "There is something there I can't quite see."

"Let's go then," Renni said. "Mahu, do you need to rest or can you manage a while longer?"

Mahu waved his hand at Renni, but didn't seem to have the strength to reply. So we walked. And walked and walked. The landscape didn't change at all. In fact, when I watched a particular shrub that was off to my left, my position in relation to it never changed, no matter how long we walked.

"We aren't going anywhere," Istnofret said at last.

"Perhaps the landscape keeps repeating like the tunnels," Renni said. "It is most strange. I can see my feet passing over the ground when I look down, but I don't actually seem to move."

"It is like when I tried to run around the Gates of Anubis," Behenu said. "No matter how far I ran, I could never get past them."

"Is this another spell?" Sabu asked.

"Or a test," I said.

"What kind of test this time?" Istnofret asked.

"I don't know," I said. "But I wonder if there is something we are supposed to do and until we figure it out, we will keep walking without going anywhere."

The idea felt right. This was a test, or another of Anubis's tricks, and there was something we had to do before he allowed us out of this endlessly repeating landscape.

"If this is a test, there must be a clue," I said. "Look around. There will be something to tell us what to do."

"But there is nothing here," Istnofret said with a sigh. She flopped down onto the grass. "We may as well sit while we think. There is no point continuing to walk."

Everyone else sat and Mahu lay down. He breathed far too heavily, considering we hadn't been walking all that fast. I remained standing to study our surroundings. Flat grassy land. Knee-high shrubs. The pale sky with the sun that still stood overhead despite the hours we had been here. The strange, almost misty sunlight. There was a clue here. I just wasn't seeing it.

Behenu passed around some food.

"This is the very last of the dried meat," she said. "And there's only a little cheese left so I think we should save that for now."

I chewed my strip of meat. It was dry and verging on rancid, but I was too hungry to throw it away.

"I cannot believe I am going to starve to death in the underworld," Sabu said as he lay back on the grass. "This is not what I expected when I asked to come with you."

Renni laughed a little, although he didn't sound amused. Something about Sabu's words made my skin tingle.

"Sabu, say that again," I said.

"Say what?"

"Exactly what you just said."

"I said I didn't expect to starve to death in the underworld."

"No," I said. "You said it wasn't what you expected when you asked to come. That is what we need to do."

They all stared at me blankly.

"We need to ask permission."

"But we didn't do that last time," Istnofret said.

"Maybe the rules are different this time," I said. "Maybe this is part of Anubis's game, to keep us from getting too comfortable by making everything different."

"So is it Anubis we need to ask permission from?" Behenu asked.

"And how would we even do that?" Istnofret added. "It is not like he is here."

"He might be," I said. "Maybe we cannot see him. Or maybe we only need to say it and he will hear us, even if he is elsewhere."

"Go on then," Istnofret said. "Obviously, it must be you who asks."

I took a deep breath. This was right, I was sure of it.

"Anubis," I called. "We come to speak with the guardian of your gates, Keeper of the Lake. Will you grant us permission to approach?"

If Anubis heard me, he made no reply. Disappointment seeped through me. I had been sure I was right.

"Perhaps he didn't hear you?" Behenu suggested.

"Try again," Sabu said. "Maybe you need to say it louder."

"Or maybe you just need to turn around." Istnofret pointed behind me.

I turned and there stood the gates. Tall and glistening black, carved with images of the jackal god.

"Were they there all along?" Sabu asked.

"Maybe they were hidden," I said. "Or maybe now we are somewhere else. Who can say?"

"It doesn't matter either way," Renni said. "We found the gates. Now let's go get Intef."

SIXTEEN

I half expected the gates to remain the same distance away even as we approached, but in only a few minutes, we stood right in front of them. I stared up at the carvings of Anubis. He held an *ankh* in one hand and a flail in the other. Last time we were here, I wondered why Anubis held those particular items and I was no closer to an answer this time. He was often depicted with those things. Had always been depicted like that.

"I suppose we knock?" Sabu asked. "That is what you did last time, right?"

I inhaled shakily. I wasn't ready yet. Needed time to figure out what to do. How to convince Keeper to let Intef leave. Whether I really had the courage to offer myself in his place.

"Go on, Samun," Istnofret said. "It has to be you."

I took another deep breath and knocked. My knocks echoed. I couldn't think. Had no idea what I would say when Keeper answered.

The gates opened, but it wasn't Keeper.

"Who knocks on the Gates of Anubis?" a young voice asked.

There she was: the child from my dream. The one who stared at Intef without expression as the gates closed between them. My daughter, only she was older than she should be.

"Meketaten?" My voice was no more than a whisper.

If my daughter knew who I was, she didn't show it. She waited, clearly trying to be patient, with one hand resting on the gate, although I didn't miss the way her forefinger tapped.

I looked into her eyes. They were just like Intef's, dark with tawny flecks. She was a female version of the boy he had been. She was born less than a year ago, but the girl standing in front of me appeared to be around five or six years and sounded even older.

"Is your name Meketaten?" My voice trembled so much that I thought she wouldn't be able to understand me.

"My name" — she drew herself up tall — "is Guardian of the Path."

It was a silly thing to be upset about, but I wanted to cry. Did she know the name I gave her on the day of her birth? Did she know she was born of a mortal woman? Was she still mortal herself?

"My name is Samun." I tried not to let my voice wobble. "I was hoping to speak with Keeper of the Lake."

She stared at me, all seriousness and duty, despite being a wisp of a girl.

"You may speak with me," she said.

"I have come to ask for Intef's release."

She barely hesitated.

"No." She started to close the gates.

"Wait." I leaned against the gates, trying to prevent her from shutting them. She might not open them again once they were closed. "Please."

She paused, leaving only the tiniest crack between the gates. One tawny-flecked eye peered out at me.

"I have made my decision," she said. "There is nothing further to discuss."

"Why is it your decision? Why is it not Keeper's decision, or Intef's?"

"I am training to be the guardian of the gate. It is my decision to make."

"I want to speak with Intef."

"You may not."

"Why?"

I brushed away the tears that threatened to fall. Somehow, I didn't think tears would sway my daughter. She was strength. She would admire strength in others. I had to look strong, even if I didn't feel it.

The tawny eye stared at me.

"Because I do not wish to allow it," she said.

"Why will you not let me see the man I love? The man I have been separated from for months?"

The tears rolled down my cheeks and I couldn't stop them. So much for being strong.

The door opened a little wider and she cocked her head as she studied me.

"You are distressed. Why?" She sounded curious rather than critical.

I could only stare at her, dumbfounded. Did she know nothing of sadness? Of human emotion? Surely she had been permitted to spend time with Intef. Surely she knew the love of her father. She must have some knowledge of emotion.

"Because I have travelled a very long way to see him," I said. "I was not able to say goodbye last time and I miss him dearly."

"So you are here to farewell him?"

Should I tell her the truth — that I came to bring Intef home — or should I lie? Would it make any difference to her?

"I have come to speak with him," I said. "I can offer you payment in exchange."

"What sort of payment?"

"Wait a moment and I will fetch it for you."

I went back to my packs, although I tried to keep an eye on her, fearing she might change her mind and close the gates. The others were silent, obviously realising the conversation was not yet finished. I fumbled through the pack containing my personal items. Where was it? At last my fingers found the bangle I brought for her. It was a pretty silver thing inlaid with sapphires. I took it back to the gates and offered it to Meketaten.

She looked at it for a long moment and I was sure she would refuse it, but then she opened the gates wider and reached for the bangle. Her fingers brushed my hand as she took it from me and my heart swelled. I had never expected to touch my daughter again. She turned the bangle around, studying it from all angles.

"You wear it on your wrist," I said. "May I show you how?"

She shrugged and held the bangle out to me. I slipped it over her right wrist, trying not to let my fingers linger on her skin.

"See how pretty it looks on you?" Tears choked my voice.

She held out her arm and studied the bangle. At length, she looked at me.

"Why do you react like that to see this thing on my arm?"

"It is called a bangle," I said. "I brought it here especially for you. I hoped I would have the chance to give it to you."

"Why?"

I couldn't tell her I was her mother. If it meant nothing to her, it would kill me. I tried to smile through my tears.

"Because I knew you were here, and I thought it would look pretty on you."

She seemed to accept my explanation and returned her gaze to the bangle.

"I like it," she announced at last.

"Does that mean you will let me speak with Intef?"

She glanced over her shoulder, as if checking nobody would overhear.

"You may speak with him briefly," she said. "Wait here."

The gates closed.

SEVENTEEN

The wait seemed interminable, but at last the gates swung open and Meketaten peered out again. She studied me and I feared she had changed her mind. Then she stepped back and Intef appeared.

He didn't look at all how I expected. Meketaten was too old, but if Intef had aged at all, it was not apparent. But something else had worn away at him. He was pale, almost grey, and I felt like I would see right through him if I looked long enough. He wore a white *shendyt*, a linen shirt and sandals. The sleeve covering his stump dangled freely. He stared at me as if he didn't know who I was.

"Intef?" My voice was tentative.

"Samun, what are you doing here?"

He didn't sound pleased to see me.

"I came... We came to bring you home."

He shook his head.

"You have wasted your time then. I cannot leave. Even if I could, I would not want to. I cannot leave her here alone."

He meant Meketaten, not Keeper.

"Does she know who you are?"

He glanced behind himself, as if checking she wasn't within hearing distance.

"I have told her, but she thinks they are mere stories. Tales of a child who was born in the underworld and could not leave. A child who had a mother and a father who loved her very much. She doesn't understand the child is her."

My heart shattered. When I handed Meketaten to Osiris, I wasn't sure he would allow her to live. But when I dreamed of her with Intef, I thought she would at least know her father's love. That she would learn what it was to be human.

"Why?" I asked. "Why doesn't she know?"

"How can I tell her she is not a goddess? I am not even sure that is true. This is a strange place and it does strange things to a person. I think she is more goddess than mortal these days. She has little desire to know what it would be like to be mortal, other than an abstract curiosity in the stories I tell her."

"Do you not love her?"

He stepped forward, allowing the gates to almost close behind him.

"Of course I love her, Samun. I love her with every fibre of my being. But I cannot tell her. It would not help her survive this place. If she is to live here, she needs to be a goddess. She does not need to know how to be mortal. It would not help her here."

"I don't understand." Tears rolled down my cheeks, and I made no effort to wipe them away. "How would it hurt her to know she was born a mortal child, even if that is not what she is now? How would it hurt her to know her parents love her?"

"She can never leave this place, Samun. It would kill her to even try. So if she is to live here, it is best for her to believe she belongs here. Agree or disagree with my decision, it makes no difference. I was the one who was here for her. I may not have been able to tell her I loved her, but I was here. Where were you?"

"That isn't fair," I said. "You know I couldn't stay."

"So tell me then, did you achieve your quest? Did you remove Ay?"

"I did. He is gone and will never return to Memphis."

He sighed. "At least it was not for nothing then."

"Will you come home, Intef? I have come — we have all come — to bring you back."

He looked over my shoulder and saw, seemingly for the first time, the others who waited some distance from the gates. He raised his hand in greeting to them.

"I cannot leave her," he said. "She needs to grow up knowing someone other than Keeper."

"But this is no place for a mortal to live," I said.

"And yet I have done it, have I not? I have lived here for however long it has been and so has she."

"Are you still mortal?"

"I believe I am, and I will stay so. But she was born in the underworld. I don't think she has ever been fully mortal since that moment. Keeper says a child born in the underworld can never leave. She won't survive away from this place."

"Why not? She was born of mortal parents. Surely she could live in the mortal realm. Does she not breathe air and need water just as we do?"

"I don't understand it," he said. "Not fully and not even almost. I only know she will die if she tries to leave. Keeper has made that quite clear."

"Maybe Keeper isn't telling the truth."

"Would you risk our daughter's life on a gamble? I have never known Keeper to be anything but honest. They may twist the truth, yes — what god doesn't? — but they have never lied to me."

I looked away, trying to steady myself. His words seemed cold, but they were also pragmatic. He could always see the core of a problem without being swayed by emotion. This was Intef as he had always been.

"So there is no possibility for her to leave?" I asked, at last.

"None." His voice was gentle now. "And I am sure you knew that even before you came here."

I nodded, unable to admit he was right. I had come to retrieve Intef, not Meketaten.

"Is my shadow's babe here?" I asked. "And her mate?"

"Yes," he said. "They are both here. As long as I am here, my shadow must stay."

My shadow would want her mate back. Did it know I intended to stay? It would have to stay, too. If I stayed and Intef left, my shadow and her mate would not be reunited.

"Surely you do not want to spend the rest of your life in this place?" I whispered.

"She needs me," he said. "She doesn't know it, but she does. Although everything I tell her is couched in terms of tales and wonders, I can teach her what she needs to know. She knows compassion, even if she only understands it on an intellectual level. She knows honesty and trustworthiness and honour. If I was not here, she would know nothing of these things."

"But how much longer do you need to stay?"

He sighed and looked up to the sky as if searching for a sign.

"Until I think she doesn't need me anymore. I don't know when that will be, and even if that time comes, Keeper might not allow me to leave. There was no end date to the agreement we made with them. Samun, you need to leave me here. Move on with your life. Now that you have finished your quest, go and... live. Find your sisters. Do something for yourself instead of always chasing after something for someone else."

"I cannot," I said brokenly. "If it was me here, you wouldn't leave me. I cannot do that to you either. This place is killing you, Intef. I wish you could see how you look. You are like a ghost."

"You must leave me." He reached out to wipe a few tears from my cheeks. His touch was gentle, and it made me cry even harder. "Our daughter needs me here, Samun, and I will stay for her."

With that, he stepped back through the gates and they swung shut behind him.

"Intef!" I called.

My knock made no noise. The gates would not open to me again.

"Intef!"

I fell to my knees, sobbing. Tears dripped between my fingers and soaked the grass.

"I cannot leave you here. You cannot stay."

But the gates didn't open.

EIGHTEEN

E ventually, somebody came to wrap an arm around my shoulders.
"Samun."

It was Istnofret.

"Samun, get up. Step away from the gates. That's right, come over here."

She led me back to the others. I couldn't look at any of them, but I heard someone — Behenu maybe — sniffling.

"He won't come?" Renni asked.

Of course, they couldn't hear our conversation from back here. Through more tears, I told them.

"She doesn't know she has parents?" Istnofret asked. "But... how..."

"I don't understand." I tried to get my tears under control, but the more I talked, the more futile it became. "He won't leave her. We came all this way for nothing."

"So that is it?" Istnofret asked. "He said no and you are going to walk away?"

I gave her a bewildered look.

"What choice do I have? I can hardly burst through the gates and drag him out."

"Maybe that is exactly what we need to do," Renni said. "If he won't come willingly, we have to extract him."

"You plan to break into a place that is guarded by a goddess and a — I don't know what she is, a junior goddess? — and steal Intef away? Drag him kicking and screaming because he doesn't want to come?"

"Or we need to convince him," Renni said, with a shrug that implied it didn't matter either way. "We came to get Intef back and I, for one, don't intend to leave without him."

"We don't have a choice, Renni," I said. "He won't leave and that is that."

"So you are going to give up on him?" Istnofret asked. "You know Intef would never give up on you. Not in a million times a million years. If it was you stuck in this place, he would spend the rest of his life plotting a way to get you back."

"But he doesn't want to leave," I said. "If he gave me any sign he wanted it, of course I wouldn't leave him here. But he told me clearly that he won't leave Meketaten or Guardian of the Path or whatever it is she calls herself. He wants to stay for her sake."

"Maybe he has to be careful of what he says," Mahu said. He was lying on the grass again, but his voice sounded a little stronger than it had before.

"You don't know whether Keeper was listening," Sabu added. "There might be things he couldn't say in front of them."

"Intef does nothing without a reason," Istnofret said. "And I don't for a moment believe he would choose to stay in this place rather than be with you."

"He is choosing to be with our daughter," I said. "Of course he would choose her over me. I would do the same myself."

I hadn't even had a chance to tell him I intended to stay in his place. Meketaten wouldn't be alone.

"Maybe he thinks he doesn't have a choice," Behenu said. "Maybe his decision is not so much a choice, but what he thinks is expected of him."

"Or maybe he is trying to make it easy for you, Samun." Istnofret's voice was gentle. "He might be trying to give you a reason to walk away."

"A minute ago, you said we should keep trying to get him. Now you think he wants me to walk away?"

"I don't know what to think," she said. "I only know Intef always has a plan. We have to figure out what he is thinking and then we will know what to do."

Renni's stomach growled, and he placed his hand over it with an embarrassed wince.

"We have nothing left but that little bit of cheese," Behenu said.

"So perhaps the decision of what to do about Intef needs to wait while we figure out where to get more supplies," Renni said. "I am sure I am not the only one who is hungry."

"We have walked a long way today," Sabu said. "Perhaps our most immediate concern must be supplies and somewhere safe to sleep. We can figure out what to do tomorrow. Nothing will change in the meantime."

There was nothing here except grass and shrubs and the Gates of Anubis. No trees with fruit, no hares, no birds. Nothing we could eat.

"Look," Behenu said. "The gates are opening."

Anticipation rose within me as I turned. Intef had changed his mind. He would leave after all. But the gates opened just enough for a basket to be pushed through. Then they closed again.

"Do you think that is for us?" Istnofret asked.

"There is nobody else here," Renni said. "I will go see what it is."

He jogged over to the gates and returned with the basket.

"Supplies." He sounded almost cheerful. "Maybe someone in there was listening or Intef figured we didn't have much left by now. Either way, there is enough food in here to last us two days."

We lay down a couple of blankets and emptied out the supplies. Behenu inspected them and returned most to the basket. The food was plain, but looked fresh. Loaves of bread, some soft cheese, a couple of handfuls of ripe figs and dates. Two stoppered flasks of wine.

I accepted a chunk of bread from Behenu and sliced off some cheese with my dagger. At least I was finally remembering to keep my dagger on my person, I thought, somewhat bitterly. Just as I was about to take a bite, Sabu called out.

"Stop," he said. "Do you think this is safe to eat? Since we are in the underworld and all."

"Intef wouldn't let them send us food we couldn't eat," I said.

"He might not know," Renni said.

I examined the bread and cheese in my hand. It looked perfectly normal. The bread was fresh and still a little warm, with an appealing aroma.

"Maybe we shouldn't eat it," Istnofret said, mournfully. "Just in case."

My stomach growled.

"We can trust that Intef wouldn't let them poison us." I took a bite before anyone could object. The bread was warm and chewy with a crisp crust. "It is good," I said around a mouthful.

"I wasn't thinking about poison," Sabu said. "I thought once we had eaten it, we might not be able to leave here or something. It is probably a stupid thought."

The bread suddenly tasted like ashes. I forced myself to swallow.

"It is too late now," I said. "I have already eaten."

"Well, if you are stuck here, then I will be stuck with you," Istnofret said and bit into her bread.

Sabu was the last to eat, but after watching the rest of us for a few minutes, it seemed he could resist no longer.

My stomach felt pleasantly full afterwards. I lay back on my blanket and looked up at the strange sky. The sun still hadn't moved in all the time we had been here, and neither had its light changed. Although I had no sense of time of day, I was very weary. I closed my eyes and drifted off.

I woke slowly, coming to awareness of the fact that I was awake only after some time. Renni and Sabu had moved away to talk. Istnofret and Mahu were asleep. Behenu was lying down, but her eyes were open. She caught my gaze and gave me a small smile.

Not knowing what to say to any of them, I pretended to sleep again. Eventually I heard someone moving around and when I opened my eyes, I found Istnofret was now awake and Behenu was up. Seeing that we were waking, Renni and Sabu came back over. Sabu gave Mahu a light kick.

"Wake up, man," he said. "You have had enough beauty sleep."

Mahu grabbed Sabu's ankle as he passed, almost tripping him, and Sabu kicked him away with a laugh.

"We have made a decision," Renni said. He looked at me and shook his head a little. "Samun, I am sorry if you disagree, but we have decided we will try to retrieve Intef."

I held my tongue. If Intef was determined to stay, there would be no changing his mind. But arguing with Renni wouldn't help.

"What is the plan then?" Istnofret asked.

"We are going to ask to speak with Keeper," he said. "If Intef will not see sense, then we will go over his head. Surely it is Keeper's decision, not his, as to whether he stays."

"What if Keeper says no?" I asked.

"We will offer a trade. See what they want in exchange for Intef."

"They will want another living soul," I said.

I held my breath for a moment, testing the words I needed to say.

"Keeper already has a soul to keep them company," Renni said. "They have Meketaten. Perhaps now they will let Intef go."

"If they need someone else to stay, I will do it," Sabu said.

My expression was probably one of horror, although I quickly tried to wipe the look off my face. Shame flooded me that someone else had been the first to offer. It should have been me.

"You cannot do that, Sabu," I said. "I won't trade Intef's life for someone else's. Anyone's. If someone else must stay, it will be me."

"I owe him a debt," Sabu said. "And if I must repay it with my life, that is no more than I owe him."

"He took a whipping for you," I said. "That doesn't oblige you to give up your life for him."

He shook his head.

"Samun, I know you mean well, but you cannot understand what something like that means to a guard. It might be just a whipping for you, but to me, it is much, much more."

"Sabu." Renni slapped him on the back. "Intef would not want this."

"Maybe it won't be necessary," Sabu said. "But if someone needs to stay in his place, I will do it. And I will look after your daughter for you," he said to me. "You do not need to fear for her. I will treat her as my own."

Unexpected tears rose to my eyes and I dashed them away. My throat was choked and I could only nod at him. If they were all determined to retrieve Intef, that was what we would do. However, if Meketaten was to live in this place without her father, she should at least have her mother with her. I wouldn't let Sabu trade himself for Intef.

NINETEEN

"Might as well get on with it then," Renni said. I folded my blanket and placed it tidily in my pack. It seemed wrong to leave our campsite messy when we were about to speak with a god, even a minor one. I tucked the necklace I brought for Keeper into my pouch. We all straightened our clothes and our hair, then went to the gates. I didn't know what I would say to Keeper to convince them to let Intef leave and for me to stay in his place.

"I suppose I should knock again?" I asked. "But what do I do if Meketaten answers? Or Intef?"

"Just ask to speak with Keeper," Istnofret said. "Say you have business with Keeper and you will not discuss it with anyone else."

I knocked, and at length, the gates opened. Keeper of the Lake's human form and leonine face were just as I remembered. I had wondered, perhaps absurdly, whether they might look different.

"So." Once again, Keeper's voice was neither male nor female, young nor old, but somehow everything all at once. "You return."

"I wondered if we might discuss the matter of Intef," I said.

They cocked their head at me.

"What matter of Intef might that be?"

"Well, the fact that he is still here. We have come to take him home."

"Surely you remember our agreement? That one of you must stay behind in order for the rest to pass through the gates?"

"If you will allow him to leave, I will stay in his place."

Somebody behind me sucked in a breath. Istnofret, maybe.

"Why would I allow such a thing?" Keeper asked. "That is not the agreement we made."

I took a deep breath. I tried to think, to come up with a persuasive argument, but my mind whirled and I couldn't think of anything to say that might convince them. Keeper waited, staring at me impassively.

"You asked for a living soul to stay," I said. "You didn't specify who it must be or that it must always be the same person. I came to trade myself for Intef."

"Why?"

"Because..." I floundered. "Because Intef is a good person. He deserves the chance to go home. To live a normal life."

"Why?"

Was that not enough? What else could I say?

"If it was me here, he would come to get me. He wouldn't give up until he had taken me home."

"But it is not you here. It is him. And we made an agreement."

"I am offering myself in his place. Surely it doesn't matter which soul stays, only that someone does?"

Time seemed to stop while Keeper studied me. My heart pounded and I couldn't quite get enough air into my lungs. At length Keeper shook their head.

"No," they said. "Not all mortals can live in this place. You are not the right type."

Relief and despair crashed over me, mingling until I could barely tell which was stronger.

"But Intef is fading away here," I said. "He cannot stay forever. I can see the change in him. This place is killing him."

Keeper only looked at me. This, it seemed, did not concern them.

"Perhaps you might exchange Intef for something of value from the mortal world then?"

It was the only other thing I could offer if they wouldn't accept me as a substitute. I wouldn't offer Sabu.

Keeper's face showed not the slightest bit of interest, although they did ask, "What kind of item?"

I pulled the necklace from my pouch. It was a delicate piece with a golden ankh suspended from a string of glass beads. I offered it to Keeper.

"This is highly desired in our world," I said. "It is a very fine item."

Keeper extended their hand, and I was surprised to see it looked human. Somehow I had expected a paw. I placed the necklace on their palm. They studied the item, then shrugged.

"What use would I have for such a thing?" they asked.

"It is a necklace. You wear it around your neck. Like this."

I reached beneath my shirt to retrieve the two necklaces I wore: the spell bottle I purchased at the bazaar and the acacia seed pod from the Syrian healer. Interest flared in Keeper's eyes.

"That one." They reached out to touch the spell bottle gently. "You may take him in exchange for that."

My fingers lingered on the little amber bottle.

"This? This isn't a normal necklace. It contains a spell to protect me. It warns me when I am in danger."

Keeper's eyes narrowed.

"That is my offer. Intef for the spell."

I slipped the cord over my neck and held it out.

"I accept."

Keeper took the bottle and offered me back the *ankh* pendant.

"Perhaps you might exchange Meketaten for that one?"

The words were barely out of my mouth before Keeper narrowed their eyes at me. I had made a mistake.

"I assume you refer to the child, although it is not known by that name here." Keeper's voice was quiet, yet in the distance thunder seemed to rumble in time with their words. "The child will not leave this place. Not now. Not ever."

"I am sorry." I took the pendant and hoped Keeper didn't see how my hands trembled. *Please, Isis, let them not change their mind about Intef.* "Will you permit Intef to leave now?"

Keeper didn't reply, and the gates began to close.

"Wait," I called. "Please, I thought we agreed."

No matter how hard I beat my fist on the gates, I made no noise. Keeper did not intend to open the gates to me again.

"Keeper, please."

Tears ran down my cheeks. I hadn't even realised I was crying. I scrubbed them away and knocked again, but still it made no sound.

Not knowing what else to do, I turned back to the others. But nobody looked at me. They all looked behind me.

I turned, my heart beating a hopeful dance. The gates had opened and Intef appeared.

"No," he said, turning back to someone behind him. "I have to stay with her. Please, you must let me stay. She cannot grow up without human company."

A pause as he listened to a reply, presumably from Keeper.

"I don't care what agreement was made," he said. "I was not consulted. We already agreed on my life in exchange for the others passing through the gates. That agreement has not changed."

Another pause.

"No, you cannot do that. I will not leave her here alone."

The gates closed, leaving Intef outside.

"Intef?"

My voice was little more than a whisper and I didn't think he would hear me, but he turned.

"What have you done?" he asked in a broken voice. "Why would you do such a thing?"

"I was trying to save you," I said through my tears. "You cannot live in this place. We came to bring you home."

"I want to be here with her. I am the only normal thing she knows. The only mortal. The only person who loves her."

"I love her, too."

"And you were not here. I am all she knows. I cannot leave. She is the reason Keeper wanted one of us to stay. They wanted a human companion for her."

"I offered to stay in your place, but Keeper wouldn't let me. I wanted you to get home, even if it was without me."

"She needs me."

"You cannot stay here, Intef. This place is killing you. Even if Meketaten cannot leave, you must."

"Our daughter cannot grow up in this place without being loved by someone."

"I will stay. I will find a way to convince Keeper and I will make sure Meketaten remembers you. She will remember you loved her."

"She doesn't even know I am her father."

He cried in earnest now. I moved closer, wanting to put my arms around him, but he flinched away from me.

His rejection hurt. If he no longer hated me for giving Meketaten to Osiris, now he hated me for taking him away from her.

"Intef, you cannot stay here."

"No, Samun," he said bitterly. "I cannot."

Hearing my name on his lips was a bitter blow. He still called me that, even though he hated me.

"You have already made the agreement and Keeper has accepted," he said. "I have no choice."

"Intef, look."

I pointed behind him to the gates that slowly opened. Meketaten stared at us. If she felt any emotion at seeing Intef so upset, she didn't show it. Intef cleared his throat as he wiped away his tears.

"Child." He dropped onto one knee so he was of a height with her. "I have to leave this place."

"I know." Her voice was placid, almost uninterested.

"I will not be able to come back."

She cocked her head to the side and studied him.

"I am not sure whether you can understand this, but I will never see you again," he said.

"Will you tell me a story?" she asked.

"Of course." Intef's voice broke and he cleared his throat. "There was once a man who had a young daughter. She was just about your age. The man knew his daughter would grow up to be someone very important. She didn't know it, though, and she didn't understand why he did some of the things he did, but he was trying to prepare her for the day when she would have to do her important job."

"What was the job?" Meketaten asked.

"She was to be a guardian. Her duty would be to see that only the souls who were supposed to enter a certain place did so, and to keep back everyone else who might want to go there. It was a very special job. Very dangerous, too. The souls who were not allowed to enter were often tricky and desperate. The girl would need to learn how to deal with them and how to protect herself from them."

I hated knowing my daughter would be in danger. I hadn't understood what it meant to be a guardian of the underworld. But a fierce pride shone inside me. My daughter was becoming a goddess. I once fancied myself to be a goddess, but she really was, or she would be.

"But the girl needed to learn how to do those things without the man," Meketaten said. "She could not do what she had to with him there. She could not learn all of what she needed to in the presence of a mortal."

Intef stared at her for a long time and swallowed hard. Her words shook him and he seemed to struggle to find a response. Perhaps Meketaten understood who he was to her better than he had known.

"He understood she was very special," Intef said at last. "And that she had to be allowed to prepare for the important job she had been given. He didn't know he was holding her back and although he didn't want to leave her, the moment he understood was the moment he accepted he had to. So the day came when the father said goodbye to his daughter. He cried as he did and his heart broke."

Intef could barely speak through his tears now, but Meketaten studied him impassively.

"Then he left," she said. "And his daughter grew up to be very good at her important job. She was wise and strong and she always made the decisions that were best for the place she guarded. And she never forgot the man who had been there with her when she was a girl."

"He never forgot her either." Intef's voice was a whisper now. "His only desire for the rest of his life was that one day, when he departed for the West, he would see her again."

Meketaten's mask slipped and I caught a glimpse of emotion. His departure upset her more than she pretended. Intef believed she didn't know he was her father, but she did, even if she didn't quite understand why that was important.

"I suppose it is time for you to leave," she said.

"I suppose it is," Intef said.

"Goodbye then."

As the gates closed, she kept her gaze on Intef. The brief flash of emotion was gone, and she looked at him as if he was a stranger. This was the moment from my dream. I hadn't realised it would be their final farewell.

"No, please." Intef raced forward to try to stop the gates, but they closed without pause. He fell to his knees in front of them.

"Guardian. Keeper. Let me back in. I need more time."

But there was no reply from within.

TWENTY

Intef remained on his knees in front of the gates for some time after they closed. I longed to comfort him, but I was the last person he would want near him right now. Eventually Renni came over.

"Up you come." He took Intef by the arm and helped him to his feet. "Come away from the gate. Let's get you a blanket to sit on and something to drink."

"I will never see her again," Intef said through his tears.

"Let's just get you away from the gates," Renni said. "Come on."

He led Intef back to where we had camped. Neither of them looked at me as they passed. I stayed by the gates to give Intef some space. I had grieved the loss of Meketaten, but I never knew her. She was a newborn babe less than an hour old when I gave her to Osiris. Intef had known her as a babe and as a young girl. His grief would be different to mine. It was undoubtedly even greater than mine.

Renni helped Intef sit down, and Behenu was ready with a mug for him. Nobody spoke and Intef didn't seem to notice Sabu or even Mahu, who he had never met. Istnofret came to stand with me.

"He hates me more than ever now," I said. "I thought I was doing the right thing."

"You couldn't have known Meketaten was here," she said. "Unless..."

She gave me a hard look.

"But I did," I said. "I dreamed of Intef holding a child on his lap. I saw the gates closing while she looked at him."

"And you planned to offer yourself in his place all along."

"I am sorry I didn't tell you."

"I don't understand," Istnofret said. "If you knew he was with Meketaten, why wouldn't you leave him here? I know you wanted him to go home, but I don't understand why you would want to part your daughter from her father."

"As long as she had one parent here, I thought perhaps it didn't matter which of us it was. I wanted him to go home."

Istnofret shook her head.

"I cannot believe you didn't tell us," she said. "That you didn't tell me. After all we have endured for you, you're still keeping secrets."

"I didn't think you would come with me if I told you," I said. "I knew I couldn't find him by myself and I thought he would need help to get home."

She searched my face, as if trying to figure out whether I told the truth this time. Then she turned and walked away.

"Istnofret," I said.

But she kept walking.

I lingered by the gates a while longer. Istnofret must have told them what I said, for I saw Renni shake his head and put his arms around her. Nobody else came to get me, although Behenu cast me a few looks. Intef sat on a blanket, a piece of bread in his hands, although he didn't seem to eat. Eventually, I made my way over to them, but I felt too uncomfortable standing there with everyone ignoring me, so I wandered off a little way. Behenu came over to me and we stood side by side in silence.

"Does everyone hate me now?" I asked when it became clear she waited for me to speak first.

"No," she said. "We are angry you kept this from us. We would have come anyway. Even if we knew you planned to stay."

Tears welled in my eyes. They were better friends than I deserved.

"I am sorry," I said.

"I understand," she said. "Sort of. I know what it is to have a path laid out for you. You felt like you couldn't share your path. For me, everyone knew mine and I couldn't tell anyone it wasn't what I wanted."

"I should have trusted you all."

"Yes. You should have. Especially Istnofret. She is the most hurt you didn't tell us."

"Does she hate me now?"

Behenu shook her head. "I don't think Istnofret could ever hate you. But she is hurting. You need to find a way to make it up to her."

"I will."

"Come on then. Renni wants to leave."

I followed her back to the others. Mahu shot me a sympathetic look, although everyone else seemed to avoid looking at me. Intef still sat with his head hanging. Somehow, I hadn't expected to see him wearing his usual clothes and with his hair neatly trimmed. Even though he looked grey and faded, he was still Intef. Blood dripped down his arm from beneath his shirt.

"Intef, you are bleeding," I said.

He stirred at last, glancing at the blood. He set the mug aside and used the stump of his other arm to push up his sleeve.

There, branded into the skin of his bicep, was a black scarab. Blood dripped from its edges and ran down his arm.

The scarab from my dream.

"Who did that to you?" Istnofret asked, raising her hand to cover her mouth.

"I will get you a bandage." Behenu already rummaged through the packs. "We have some honey and thyme, too, which will help with the pain."

"Why, Intef?" I asked. "Why would they do that?"

"It was Keeper's parting gift to me." His tone held both bitterness and irony. "I assume it signifies something, but they didn't explain."

"I dreamed of it," I whispered. "The scarab, burned into skin, dripping blood. I saw it."

There was silence at my words. I supposed it was the wrong time to mention something else I hadn't told them.

"Do you know what it means?" Istnofret asked at last.

"No and I didn't know it had anything to do with Intef. There was no context, just the black scarab dripping with blood."

Was this another of Anubis's games? Or did Keeper play some game of their own? Perhaps the scarab would be important somehow. It might be a clue.

Behenu knelt beside Intef while she smeared honey on the scarab, then wrapped a length of linen around his bicep.

"Let me know if the blood soaks through the bandage and I will put a clean one on," she said. "We have to make sure it doesn't fester."

"We should move on," Renni said.

"Intef, do you know how to get out of here?" Sabu asked.

Intef seemed to notice him for the first time. He gave both Sabu and Mahu a somewhat puzzled look.

"This is Mahu," Renni said. "We shared a prison cell and he helped us escape. You know Sabu, of course. Tuta came, too, but he fell through the ruins and we haven't found him again yet."

If Intef wondered why any of them had come, he didn't ask.

"I know nothing about what is on this side," he said. "I only know inside the gates and around the Lake of Fire. You cannot get to the Lake without passing through the gates, so that way is shut off to us."

"So there must be another way," Renni said.

"We may as well start walking," Sabu said as he picked up some packs. "Perhaps something will occur to us on the way."

"Which way then?" Renni asked. He glanced at Intef. "Is there anything at all you know that might help us?"

Intef cast his gaze over the landscape and shrugged.

"That way, I suppose." He tipped his chin in the direction he was looking. "There is something off in the distance there, although I don't know what."

Renni shaded his eyes with his hand as he peered in the direction Intef indicated.

"What do you see?" he asked. "I see nothing but grass."

"There is a shimmer in the air. I don't know what it is."

"I don't see a shimmer."

Intef shrugged. "You stay in this place long enough, you learn to see things you didn't see before. All I can tell you is that something lies in that direction."

"Let's go then," Renni said. "Going there is the only way we will find out what it is."

"Perhaps it is the ruins?" Istnofret suggested.

"It is nothing of our world," Intef said, rather curtly.

We walked for some time and although I kept watching for the shimmer, I couldn't see anything.

"Are you sure we are getting closer?" Behenu asked. "I still don't see it."

Intef had been walking with his head hanging down. He didn't even look up.

"Keep going," he said.

TWENTY-ONE

U nlike before, when we didn't cross the plainlands no matter how long we walked, we seemed to make progress this time. I watched a few shrubs, noting how we drew closer and then passed them. When I looked behind me, the shrub was still there.

Then suddenly, in the time it took me to blink, we stood in front of an enormous building. It was so tall I couldn't see the roof. White-plastered walls. Doors set at regular intervals. There were no gardens or shady trees out the front. Just an enormous building.

"Is it a temple?" Istnofret asked.

"Or a palace maybe?" Behenu said.

We all looked at Intef, but he only shrugged.

"I told you I didn't know what was here."

"So, what do we do now?" Sabu asked. "Do we just go in?"

"It would be more polite to knock first," Istnofret said. "This could be someone's home."

"Is this another gate?" Sabu asked. "Another guardian?"

We studied the doors.

"Do you think it matters which one we choose?" Behenu asked.

The door closest to me was smooth-planed wood, so finely made I could barely see where the panels joined. In the exact centre was a wooden door knob, just the right size for a human hand to grasp. I went to the next door, which was about the length of two men away.

This one was made of bronze bars melted and twisted into the shape of a creature I didn't recognise. The next door seemed to be fashioned from sheets of bark pulled right off some enormous tree, with no care given to shape or smooth the surface.

I walked further and each door was entirely different, each one some fabulous design I had never seen the likes of. There must be some significance in the different doors. Another of Anubis's games, I presumed. I returned to the others.

"We need the right door," I said. "Anubis intends for us to go through a particular one."

"But how in the name of the goddess do we know which is the right one?" Istnofret asked.

"Split up," Renni said. "Some of us can check the doors down this way and some go that way. See if you can find anything that might suggest we should choose a particular one."

We set off along the length of the building, except for Intef, who stayed where he was, still with his head hanging down. He seemed entirely uninterested in the matter of which door we should select. I wanted to suggest he should help, that it might make him feel better if he actually did something, but kept my mouth shut. I had a feeling he wouldn't want to hear anything from me right now.

"There is an ankh carved into the corner of this door," Behenu called. "Right at the bottom. It is very small."

I looked more closely at the door in front of me.

"There are a bunch of tulips at the bottom of this one," I said.

"I have a snake eating its own tail," Istnofret called.

"I see a silhouette of Anubis," Mahu said.

"This door has an eye," Sabu said. "Perhaps it symbolises the Eye of Horus?"

We regrouped back in the centre where Intef still stood.

"What happens if we choose the wrong one?" Istnofret asked.

They all looked at me. I shrugged.

"I think this is no different to the tunnels or trying to cross the plainlands," I said. "We have thought all along that someone was controlling our path. Perhaps the other doors will simply lead us back out here again. Perhaps they will take us somewhere we don't want to go."

"Which one do we choose then?" Renni asked. "Are any of those symbols more meaningful to us than others?"

"I suppose it must be the eye," I said. "All those images are meaningful in some way, but we spent so long searching for the Eye of Horus that surely that must be the door we are supposed to choose."

"No, it is not."

Intef's voice was so quiet I wasn't sure I heard him correctly.

"This door is the one we need."

He pointed to the one we stood in front of, the one made of finely carved wood. I bent down to examine the tiny carving in the bottom corner. It was a scarab.

"Keeper was trying to help," Behenu said with a small smile. She, more than any of us, was always pleased to think the best of someone.

"Funny way to go about it," Sabu muttered. "Must have been another way they could have conveyed a message without branding Intef."

"We have the information we need," Renni said. "And I agree with Behenu that it seems Keeper was trying to help us in their own way. We know little about the rules of this place. Perhaps they were not allowed to tell us directly. Burning that image onto Intef's arm might have been the only thing they could think of in the time they had before he left."

"I still think we should knock," Istnofret said. "Just because we know this is the door we are supposed to go through doesn't mean we know who or what is on the other side."

Renni gestured for me to step forward, but I shook my head.

"I am not doing it this time."

He frowned at me.

"It should be you," he said.

"No, somebody else needs to do it."

I had made enough of a mess of trying to retrieve Intef. Let someone else see if they could do a better job. Eventually, Behenu stepped forward.

"I will do it."

Before anyone could disagree, she knocked. The movement pushed the door open slightly.

"It isn't locked." She pushed the door open a little more. "Maybe we are supposed to go in."

We waited, but nobody came to answer her knock.

"Knock again," Istnofret said. "Maybe they didn't hear last time."

Behenu did, but still nobody came. She pushed the door open all the way and we peered in.

The chamber was completely dark and I could make out nothing.

"I will find a lamp," Renni said.

"No," I said. "I think we are meant to go into the dark."

He sighed.

"Of course we are. I will go first then."

He stepped into the chamber, and the darkness immediately swallowed him.

"Renni?" Istnofret leaned in, trying to see into the chamber without setting foot inside. "Renni, what is in there?"

He didn't reply. We looked at each other.

"We cannot leave him to go by himself," Istnofret said.

"We don't know what is in there," Mahu said. "We don't know whether it is safe to follow. Something might—"

"Yes, Mahu, I know," she said. "Something might have happened to him. That is why we need to follow him immediately. If something has happened to Renni, we will need to save him."

With that, she walked into the chamber. Like Renni, she was gone immediately.

"I will go next," Behenu said and stepped forward.

Intef still stood with his head down and seemed completely unbothered by three of our friends disappearing. I looked at Mahu and Sabu. Sabu nodded at me.

"You do not need to say it," he said. "You go next. We will see that he follows."

So I stepped into the chamber. As the darkness folded in around me, for a moment I felt weightless. Then I fell.

TWENTY-TWO

I could see nothing around me but darkness. I didn't even know how big the area I fell through was. All I could do was hold on to my packs and wait to hit the ground. Another of Anubis's tricks?

I fell for a long time.

This was going to be bad.

Then I was no longer falling. I lay on my back, although I had no memory of hitting the ground. I didn't hurt. Surely I should be dead after such a fall.

Maybe I was. That would explain why my landing wasn't painful.

Beside me, Istnofret groaned and sat up. On the other side of her sat Renni.

"I suppose that wasn't as bad as I might have expected," she said.

"Are we dead?" I asked.

"I have no idea."

A groan from nearby indicated Behenu's location.

"Where are the others?" She sat up and rubbed the back of her head as if expecting it to be sore.

"They were coming after me," I said.

Someone behind me moved. It was Mahu, sitting up and shaking his head. Then Intef and Sabu were there too.

"I am sure they weren't there a moment ago," Istnofret said.

"We are all here now and I suppose that is all that matters," I said.

It was only now that I looked around. The chamber in which we landed was lit by an iridescent sheen, an almost silvery light.

"Where is the light coming from?" Behenu asked.

"It is neither candle nor lantern." Renni got to his feet slowly, as if checking for injuries. "Nor fire. I have never seen anything like it before."

"We must still be in the underworld then." Istnofret sighed. "I hoped we had somehow fallen back into our own world, like when we jumped into the Lake of Fire."

"So what now?" Sabu looked like he was trying to act casual, but his eyes were round.

"I suppose we keep walking," Renni said. "Until whoever is leading us gives us another clue."

Intef still lay on his back. I might have hoped he would think of something useful, but he wasn't making any effort to get up and likely wasn't even listening.

"Come on, man." Renni held out his hand to Intef. "Up you get."

Intef allowed Renni to haul him up, although he still didn't speak. I picked up my packs and waited for someone to decide what direction we should go in.

"I don't think there is anywhere to walk to," Istnofret said. "We seem to be in a chamber of some sort."

She was right. We had enough light to see that the area in which we arrived seemed to be enclosed. There were no doors or windows. We were trapped in here until someone came to release us.

"Maybe the door is invisible." Behenu's voice was hopeful.

"We have seen stranger things." Renni set his packs down again. "Maybe you should all wait here. We don't know if there might be some hidden danger. I will feel around the walls and see if there is a concealed exit."

The walls should have been less than two dozen paces away, but Renni kept walking. At length, he stopped and shook his head.

"It is mighty strange, but I don't think the walls are really there," he said. "It is an illusion. It is much larger than it seems."

"Perhaps we should tie ourselves together again," Sabu said. "This seems like a place where we might easily become separated."

He retrieved some string from a pack and we all fastened ourselves to it before we set off. As usual, Renni took the lead, followed by Istnofret and Behenu. Intef was behind her with me, then Sabu and Mahu at the rear. I figured Renni had placed Intef ahead of me hoping he might protect me if necessary, but also put Sabu directly behind me in case he didn't.

We only walked for a few minutes before Sabu stopped. I stopped too, unable to move forward without dragging him.

"Mahu is gone," Sabu said.

I turned to look, images of being hunted in my dream running through my mind. Sabu was correct: Mahu was gone. It couldn't have been the beast, though. This was nothing like my dream where we were running and the beast was chasing us. Could this be another test or trick?

"The string is intact," Sabu said. "It is simply untied."

"Perhaps he stopped to rest," Istnofret said, although it was clear from her voice she didn't believe it.

"He would not untie himself," Renni said. "And he wouldn't just stop without telling us."

"Where is he then?" she asked. "How could something happen to him without anyone noticing?"

"Sabu, did you hear anything?" Renni asked.

"Not a thing. There was no disturbance and Mahu never made a sound. All I noticed was a gust of wind and I turned to see where it came from. Then I realised he was gone."

"What do we do now?" Behenu asked. "Should we wait in case he comes back?"

"We keep saying someone is leading us," I said. "Anubis, maybe. If he has taken Mahu, he will return him to us once…"

I didn't know whether to say once he was finished with him or once Mahu had done whatever they wanted. Nobody seemed to notice I hadn't finished.

"Maybe he has gone to wherever Tuta is," Behenu said. She sounded hopeful, as if cheered by the thought they might be together.

"We should keep going," Renni said. "We have waited a few minutes already. Mahu will find us again if he can."

We continued walking. I kept darting glances back at Sabu and I wasn't the only one. Then I felt a puff of wind against my back. I stopped. The others ahead of me halted when the string connecting us tightened. I turned, but I already knew what I would see: Sabu was gone and the string that had tied him to us dangled freely.

"How did they get him?" Frustration filled Renni's voice. "I saw him only a moment ago."

"As did I," Istnofret said.

"There was a breeze," I said. "Just like he noticed when Mahu disappeared."

They all looked at me. I knew what they must be thinking, for I had the same thought: I was now at the end of the line. If whoever it was came again, I would be the next to be taken.

"Samun, we will tie your other hand to my free hand," Renni said. "Then we will be in a circle and nobody will walk alone at the end."

I felt better at that. Renni tied me to himself and we set off again.

In between one breath and the next, I blinked.

Then everyone else was gone.

TWENTY-THREE

I stood in a vast hall lit by hundreds of torches. The air should have
been hot and thick with their smoke, but it was the perfect tempera-
ture. Along one wall was a row of baboons. They sat on their haunches
and stared at me with eyes that glittered in the torchlight, just as they
had in my dream.

There were no doors or window, just the torches and the baboons
and a piece of golden linen about the width of my shoulders stretching
across the floor. Not knowing what else to do, I followed its path. As I
crossed the hall, an enormous throne became visible on the far side.
From this distance, I couldn't make out who sat on it. I knew this place,
though, from the pictures in the Book of Amduat. This was the Hall of
Osiris and no doubt the figure who sat on the throne was Osiris himself.

As I drew closer, my feelings were conflicted. Osiris gave me the Eye
of Horus, which I needed in order to remove Ay from the throne. But he
also took my daughter and gave her to Keeper. I was both grateful and
resentful towards him. My resentment was unfair, perhaps, given Meketaten couldn't have left the underworld, anyway. At least Osiris had
ensured her safety.

It was indeed Osiris who sat on the throne. He looked just as I remembered: green-faced and clothed in white with a tall white crown. I dropped to my belly. He was a god, after all.

"Rise."

His voice gave no clue of what he thought about my presence, but he didn't seem surprised. I had thought Anubis was the one controlling our path, but could it be Osiris?

"So Ankhesenamun, once Queen of Egypt and Lady of the Two Lands, you come finally to my Hall," he said.

"Someone took me from my friends and brought me here."

He looked at me impassively. The way his eyes glittered reminded me of something, but I couldn't quite recall what. Something important. Something I had forgotten.

"You used the Eye of Horus," he said.

So perhaps I was here because he wanted an accounting of how I used the Eye. Perhaps I was to be judged on whether it was a good or bad use of such a powerful artefact.

"I did, and I have done exactly what I intended," I said. "I have removed a dishonourable man from the throne."

"That is not what you said you would use it for."

I could only blink at him. What had I told him? It had been my intention all along to remove Ay. Surely I would not have told him something else? I wouldn't have lied to a god.

"You said you intended to restore peace to Egypt," he said. "Have you done that?"

That had indeed always been my ultimate aim, but I had thought removing Ay would make it happen. I had almost forgotten the letter which arrived from the Hittite princess Muwatti just before we left Egypt. She said the compensation I sent to her father, Suppiluliumas, had angered him and he still intended to seek vengeance for his son's death.

"Have you?" he asked again.

"I thought I had, but I have recently learned there is more to be done."

"Perhaps you were unwise in your use of the Eye."

I didn't agree, but I was certain I should keep my opinion to myself.

"Once you removed Pharaoh, you installed yourself on the throne."

His voice was emotionless. This was an observation and I couldn't tell what he thought of my actions.

"I lost myself in the Eye's call," I said. "It spoke to me of power and glory, and while I was under its influence, I wanted that power and glory for myself. I did not act in a manner befitting the Queen of Egypt."

He likely already knew. Lying, or trying to conceal anything, would win me no favour. Here, in the Hall of Osiris, the truth must always be told.

"And what do you intend to do now you have put a new pharaoh on the throne?" he asked.

"As you have already pointed out, I have yet to restore peace between Egypt and Hattusa. I still need to do that."

"You have had much help along the way."

Again, it was an observation, not a judgement.

"I have very loyal friends who have travelled all the way across the known world and even twice into the underworld with me. I could not have achieved what I did without them."

"It was not your mortal friends I referred to."

Who then? Keeper? Again the voice whispered in my ear: *Be careful of the jackal.* Did Osiris refer to whoever told me that? Or maybe he meant Anubis?

"There have been others who helped me on the way," I said. "I am grateful to all of them."

"Have you ever regretted your decision?"

"At times, yes. The journey was difficult, and we lost much along the way. My two babes. Intef's arm. Our friend, Tuta, who disappeared before we entered the tunnels. We don't know whether he is safe."

"I meant your decision to return."

"Return to the underworld?"

"Return to life."

At first I didn't understand, but then a memory formed in my mind. A world without colour. An endless beach. Waves that made no sound. Falcon eyes glittering.

I had drowned and Horus gave me a choice: I could go on to Osiris's Hall or I could return to life. I made the decision for both Meketaten, who was yet unborn, and myself. Horus had said that if I didn't return to my life, Meketaten would have no chance at an afterlife, since she had not yet drawn breath. I decided to go back, and I drowned a second time. Had Horus known when he gave me those options that Meketaten would not lead a normal life?

"I chose life for both of us," I said. Would it have been better for Meketaten had I chosen otherwise?

"Your quest would have remained incomplete had you not."

He seemed faintly approving.

"Why didn't I remember until just now?" I asked.

"Some things are not meant to be remembered. Some things you will remember when the time is right."

"I am very grateful to have been given the chance to return. To complete my quest. To…" My voice broke and I took a deep breath. "I am also grateful you allowed Meketaten to live. I thought you might… dispose of her."

"You thought I would kill the babe you traded for the Eye of Horus?"

His expression seemed cold now. Perhaps I imagined his previous approval.

"Will she always stay with Keeper?" I asked. "Will she be a guardian of the gate one day?"

"She is already a guardian. She watches for mortal souls who wander where they should not and guides them back to their own world. Only one who was born mortal can undertake such a task."

"So Keeper was mortal once?" I asked. "They had a human mother?"

"Keeper, too, was born in the underworld. Like your daughter, they can never leave."

"Keeper doesn't… they don't look human."

"They are not. They have been in the underworld for too long."

"Will my daughter look like that one day?"

"Perhaps. Perhaps not. Your daughter controls her appearance. It is up to her how she presents herself."

"Is that why she looks older than she should? I thought time might pass differently here."

"There is no time here. It neither passes nor not."

"My dreams," I said. "Why do I sometimes dream of what may come from my decisions? And why do things never work the way I try to make them?"

He stared at me for so long I thought he wouldn't answer, but at last he did.

"You surely do not expect to harness such an ability without effort?" he asked.

"Harness? Do you mean I can control my dreams?"

"Apparently not, but then what effort have you made to learn to do so? To make them show you what you want to see?"

"I didn't know I could learn to control them. Who would teach me such a thing?"

"That is something you will need to discover for yourself."

So there were limits to how much information he intended to give me.

"Are my friends safe?" I asked. "Two of them were taken before I was."

"Your friends, like you yourself, will be judged."

"I don't understand."

"You think to come to my Hall and not be judged? This is the place of judgement. All who enter this Hall will be judged."

"But we are not dead."

"And yet you came here anyway."

"We were brought here."

He raised his hands, palm up, as if to say *what of it*?

"I thought a person could only be judged if they had been embalmed," I said.

"Yet here you are."

"Is my judgement finished then? Will I be permitted to return to my friends?"

He made a noise that might have been a laugh.

"Your judgement has yet to begin."

Osiris pointed behind me.

Where before had been nothing, now stood an enormous gold scale. One arm tipped downwards while the other pointed up. I didn't need the Book of Amduat to know what this was. Every Egyptian child was raised with knowledge of the judgement they would face when they reached the Hall of Osiris.

"I am to have my heart weighed against the Feather of Truth?" I asked.

"I trust you understand the consequences?"

In the time I had been looking at the scale, a fearsome beast appeared beside him. She had the head of a crocodile while her body was a mix of lion and hippopotamus. Ammut the Devourer would eat my heart if it proved to be heavier than the Feather of Truth. Behind the Devourer appeared the judges. There was no need to count them; there would be forty-two. I turned back to the scales and there stood Anubis, the jackal-headed god, the one somebody had warned me was a trickster. Beside him waited ibis-headed Thoth, whose duty it was to record the results of the weighing of the heart. My legs trembled as I turned back to Osiris.

"But I am still alive," I said. "I will die if you take my heart to weigh it."

"Something you should perhaps have considered before you entered my Hall. Go now, it is time."

TWENTY-FOUR

Anubis gestured for me to approach. His jackal face gave no indication of his thoughts. He is a trickster, I reminded myself. He won't actually kill me in order to take my heart. It is all a trick.

I didn't believe it, though. I should run away. Yell. Cry at least. But all I could do was walk towards him. I stopped just in front of Anubis and bowed my head. It was better than looking into his strange face. I had lived my whole life surrounded by images of the gods, but it was still disturbing to come face-to-face with them, to look into their animal eyes and yet see arms and hands and legs and feet that looked as human as mine.

Anubis loomed over me, then he plunged his hand into my chest and pulled out my heart. It continued to beat even as he carried it over to the scale.

I pressed my hands against my chest, expecting a gaping hole. Perhaps if I could stem the blood, I might live long enough for him to return my heart. But my chest was whole and I felt no pain. Anubis had removed my heart right out from under my skin and bones. I could feel it beating still, but it was over there in his hand, not in my chest.

He placed my heart in the bowl that hung from the uppermost arm of the scale. The scale's balance shifted and the bowl sank. As the other bowl rose, I caught sight of the Feather: it was a tiny thing, no larger than a downy feather from a chick, yet it had been heavy enough to hold the scale's arm down.

I could barely breathe as the scales tipped and the bowls swung. The bowl containing my heart dipped down lower, but then it swung back up and the feather's bowl went lower. Up and down they swung. When they stopped, the two bowls were at an even height.

"Hmm," Anubis said.

"My heart is no heavier than the Feather of Truth," I said, a little desperately.

Ammut licked her lips, as if anticipating a meal. If Anubis gave my heart to the Devourer, that would be the end of me. I would not return to life and nor would I have an afterlife. I would be gone.

"Neither is your heart lighter than the Feather," Anubis said. "As is required in order to pass the test."

"Everything I have done has been for Egypt," I said. "I did not act for my own benefit."

I supposed this was when I was supposed to recite the Negative Confessions. We princesses were all drilled in them from our earliest school years.

I have not lied.

I have not stolen.

I have not killed.

But none of them were true.

I have not been sullen.

I have not lost my temper.

I have not been deaf to the truth.

I had done them all.

"I have lied." My voice shook. "I promised Hemetre I would release her son as soon as I was in a position to do so, but I didn't. I used the Eye of Horus to steal the throne from the man who called himself Pharaoh because I didn't accept his claim to it. I killed a man with my own hand by driving a knife into his belly while he lay in my bed."

All the Negative Confessions — all the things I was supposed to say I hadn't done — I had done all of them.

As I spoke, the bowl containing my heart sank.

"I pretended to be a goddess, and I ignored those who tried to tell me otherwise. I ordered the deaths of four men who tried to kill my friends and I. I broke the promises I made to my shadow. I withheld the truth about this journey from my friends. I didn't tell them I intended to offer myself in exchange for Intef, and I didn't tell them that one of us will die."

The bowl sank even further. With so many wrongdoings, my heart was far heavier than the Feather. Was there any way to redeem myself?

"What justification do you offer for your sins?" Osiris asked, when I finished my accounting of the Negative Confessions.

I turned back to him, although it meant Anubis was now behind me. Somehow I didn't think he was a god I should let out of my sight.

"I was trying to protect my friends, my people, my country," I said. "I have done the best I could. The decisions I made were what I thought was right in that moment. I realise now they were not always the best decisions I could have made."

"Your decisions may have been what you thought were right at the time, but what did you do when you learned they were not?" he asked.

In truth, I never thought I would be called on to justify my actions, not until after I died at any rate. I hadn't expected my judgement to come so soon. If I lied now, that would add one more fault to my tally.

"I did eventually release Hemetre's son," I said. "Once I came to my senses and was no longer in the grip of the Eye, I sent him home, along with two gems for his mother so they could live in luxury for the rest of their lives. I stole the throne because I thought I knew what my people needed better than the man who stole it from me. As for the man I killed in my bed, I saved him from a worse fate. Also, he had threatened to kill others before they could kill him. Some of those might have been people I cared about. I acted both for his sake and for the sake of those I loved."

"So you admit to your sins?" Osiris asked. A murmuring rose amongst the judges, and he held up one hand for silence. "Tell me why the Devourer should not receive your heart."

"Take my heart if you must." I drew myself up tall and looked him in the eyes. "But I beg you to allow my friends to return to the mortal world. They are here only out of love for me, and for Intef, who we came to retrieve. They would not have ventured back into this place for any other reason. If you must take my heart, let it serve as punishment for that which any of my friends are found deserving of."

Osiris looked behind me and I turned to see the scales had moved again. My heart was higher than the Feather of Truth by just the tiniest bit. Hope bubbled up inside of me.

Anubis studied the scales, his head cocked to one side as he waited for them to move again. Our eyes met briefly. He had the assessing gaze of a predator. *He is a trickster,* the voice I once heard said again. Was it possible that Anubis manipulated the scales?

The scales stayed as they were, with my heart just a little higher than the Feather. Thoth set his reed pen against his scroll, ready to record the outcome. At last, Anubis looked over at the judges.

"What say you?" he asked. "Do you find the mortal worthy or not worthy?"

The judges spoke between themselves. I could hear nothing of what they said. Even if they condemned me, maybe I could still save my friends.

One of the judges rose.

"We would like to hear more of the mortal's justifications for her actions. She has only accounted for half the sins she confessed to."

I took a shaky breath. I could hardly remember what else I had said.

"I let the Eye seduce me," I said. "It told me I was a goddess and that I should be worshipped. One of my friends tried to tell me I wasn't and I had him locked away. I threatened to execute another friend, one who is very dear to me, because she tried to tell me I was wrong."

I paused to gather my thoughts. The judges were silent while they waited and if they were at all favourably inclined towards me, I got no sense of it. Anubis studied me with his jackal eyes. Osiris, too, watched, his eyes glittering in the torchlight. Ammut stared at me, her mouth open and her tongue hanging out. Likely she was thinking about how tasty my heart might be. Only Thoth never looked at me, but continued to study the scroll in his hands as he waited to record the outcome of my judgement.

"Once I realised I was not in fact a goddess, I tried to atone for my actions," I said. "I released those I had imprisoned unfairly and gave them restitution. I told my friend she need not fear I would execute her.

I abdicated the throne and gave it to the man who my brother had named as heir, and I kept my promise to my mother's sister that she would be queen after me.

"As for the four men I ordered killed, they had already tried to kill us, and they would have tried again if we let them live. I suppose we should have handed them over to the authorities so they could face trial, but the risk of escape was too high. I did what I thought was necessary to protect myself and my friends, and I would do the same again."

That was probably not what the judges wanted to hear. I might have just doomed myself.

"And what of your promises to your shadow?" the judge asked.

My shadow. How many times had I forgotten?

"I promised to talk to my shadow," I said. "I promised to remember that it was its own being. That even if I could not hear it speak or see it move on its own, I knew it could think and feel. But I keep forgetting."

I paused, searching for an explanation. They all waited.

"I cannot defend my actions towards my shadow," I said, at last. "There is no excuse for how I have treated it. I promised to remember, but I didn't. My shadow has been with me my whole life and I have never paid it any attention. I kept forgetting it was an independent being. It was just like it had always been: always there, always silent, moving only when I did. I did not put enough importance on remembering my promises to it. I failed my shadow and I have no excuse for my actions."

"What would you do differently if you had the chance?" the judge asked.

"I would like to apologise to my shadow," I said. "And I would try harder to remember to talk to it every day. No, I would not just try. I would find a way to remember, even if it meant branding a reminder along my arm. I would make sure I always kept my shadow in the front of my mind and I would consider how my actions would impact on it."

"Like when you gave me your daughter?" Osiris asked. "Did you ever consider that you were also giving up your shadow's daughter?"

"Whether or not I considered it, it would not have changed my actions," I said. "You made it very clear that she was the price for the Eye. I needed the Eye to complete my quest, and if I had to give up not only my daughter but also someone else's, I would do it again. I have a responsibility towards my people. Towards my country."

"Do you not also have a responsibility towards your daughter?" he asked.

I took my time in answering.

"As much as I would rather have my daughter with me, that she grow up in the mortal world, that she live as a normal girl, who am I to say the life ahead of her is less than what she would have had? She will be a goddess. A guardian. She will shepherd mortals back to their own world. She will stop the creatures of the underworld from leaving this place. The importance of such a task cannot be understated. My heart is selfish and it longs for my daughter to return to the mortal world with me, but I know she is far too important for such a thing."

I waited, but it seemed there were no further questions. The scales had not moved in all the time I was giving my justification. At last, Anubis looked back towards the judges.

"So," he said. "What is your decision?"

One of the judges rose. I held my breath and clasped my hands together so nobody would see how they shook. Had I done enough?

"We find the mortal worthy," the judge said.

TWENTY-FIVE

Anubis studied me for what felt like a very long time. Would he reject the judges decision? But he took my heart from the bowl and held it, considering. Then he came to me and pushed it back into my chest.

For a moment, I felt nothing. Then came the blessed sensation of my heart beating within my chest, pushing my blood through my veins.

"Thank you." I turned to the judges. "Thank you all."

A couple nodded at me, but most only stared impassively.

"Am I free to leave?" I asked Osiris.

"You may," he said.

"And my friends?"

"It depends on their judgements. If they are found worthy, they may leave. If not…"

He cast a pointed glance towards Ammut, who waited at his side as if she were a loyal hound, not a fearsome beast.

"Before you leave, though." Osiris held out his hand. "You have used the Eye and cannot use it again. Give it to me so I may keep it safe."

"Why do you guard it? It is supposed to be Horus's own eye, so why does he not look after it himself?"

"You presume much, mortal. What right do you have to ask the business of the gods?"

"I am sorry. I did not mean to offend."

"The Eye remains with me to ensure it is not handed over too freely. It should be used only for matters of the highest importance."

And Horus had given it to mortals for the sake of a woman. Perhaps the gods didn't trust him to judge the appropriate moment to allow the Eye to be used.

"Give it to me," Osiris said.

"I have it here." I fumbled for my pouch, which, thank Isis, was at my waist where it should be. I retrieved the Eye and rested it on the palm of my hand. It slept now, dormant perhaps. "It hasn't spoken to me since I used it."

Osiris held out his hand.

"Pass it to me. I cannot take it from you."

I handed him the Eye with trembling fingers.

"Go now. Before the judges regret their decision."

Between one blink and the next, it all disappeared. Osiris, the judges, Ammut, the Hall. I stood once again in darkness. The area felt small and claustrophobia rose within me. My dream of being hunted through the tunnels was vivid in my mind and I imagined I felt the beast's breath on my neck. I stretched out my arms and took hesitant steps, searching for a wall. If I had my back to the wall, I would be safer. The beast could not sneak up behind me that way.

A popping feeling as if something tore away.

An icy touch to my hand.

"Shadow?"

The touch was gone. I had no sense of a presence, but surely it was my shadow. Was this an accident or had the judges given me an opportunity to follow through on what I said?

"Shadow, are you still there?"

No response, but of course my shadow had never spoken to me, not using words at any rate. It communicated with hand signals and body language. If I couldn't see my shadow, I had no way of knowing what it might want to say, but it could still hear me.

"Shadow, I am so sorry I didn't speak to you enough. I did not mean to forget you."

I didn't need sight to know what my shadow would be doing right now. When it was upset with me, it would huff and turn its back and cross its arms.

The icy touch came again, this time on my belly.

I took a deep breath. This was probably the thing most unforgivable for my shadow.

"I am so sorry, but I had no choice. She was the payment. Without her, Osiris wouldn't have given me the Eye, and without the Eye, I couldn't do what I needed to. But you had no share in my decision and for that, I am truly sorry. I don't know whether you might have found some other way if you had the chance. Perhaps you would have chosen to stay with your babe. I know my quest meant nothing to you. I did what I thought was best, but I regret I didn't consult you first. We should have decided together."

The icy touch came to my belly again, longer this time, lingering. Did it indicate forgiveness? Perhaps my shadow understood? Even agreed, maybe? I had not expected that. But then, its babe was born in the underworld, just like mine. Neither of our daughters could leave this place. If my shadow stayed here with its babe, we would be separated forever. I couldn't be resurrected without my shadow, but I had no idea what expectations for the afterlife a shadow might have. Perhaps this was not a consideration for it.

"I am sorry, too, that you have been parted from your mate. I hope the two of you can be reunited now we have retrieved Intef."

If Intef passed his judgement. Like me, he wouldn't be able to say the Negative Confessions. He had killed; he had lied. Always to protect me, but would the judges think that sufficient justification?

"Will you come back to me, Shadow? Will you join with me? You know I cannot leave this place if you and I are not united. After all we have endured for the ones we love, surely you would not want us to stay here without them?"

My shadow didn't reply, not even a touch of its hand. Was that a rejection?

"Please, Shadow. I need to find my friends. I suppose we are in the tunnels and I cannot stay here. There is danger in this place. I am sure you know it as well as I do. We have to find them and tell them before it is too late."

I should have been honest with them from the start. I should have told them I intended to offer myself in exchange for Intef and I should have told them about the beast. One of us would die regardless of whether they knew ahead of time. But at least they would know. I should have given them that much, rather than presuming to decide for them.

"I promise to talk to you more. I haven't done a very good job of remembering. You have no reason to trust me, but please believe that I mean it. I will do better this time."

My shadow didn't reply. I pleaded and used every argument I could think of. I cried, I begged. But my shadow didn't respond.

"Shadow, are you still there?"

I would know if it had rejoined me. Surely I would know if it had left?

When I ran out of words, there was nothing else to do but move on. I needed to find my friends. I wouldn't know whether my shadow was still here until I found a light source.

"Shadow, I need to search for my friends, and I hope you will come with me. I don't think either of us can survive if we are separated."

There was still no reply, so I began to walk.

TWENTY-SIX

The darkness was absolute. I slid my feet along the floor so I wouldn't trip, one hand on the wall and one held out in front of me. I reached a turn and followed the tunnel left. In the darkness, something moved.

I froze. The beast had found me. But whatever it was didn't seem interested in me. Its passage along the rocky floor was no more than a whisper accompanied by a soft hiss. I couldn't move for fear I would step on it or trip over it. Behind me, another creature approached. Ahead of me, one hissed.

Then they were all around me.

One slithered over my foot, its cool body rough against my skin. Another wound around my ankle.

I couldn't move.

I couldn't breathe.

They were everywhere.

Slithering over the walls and the floor.

Up my legs, across my arms, down my back.

One wound around my neck. Its head nestled against my shoulder and its tongue tasted my skin.

Another explored my hair.

Light flared, blinding me. When my eyes adjusted, the sight of the snakes was even more terrifying than not being able to see them. I recognised viper and cobra, but the rest were unknown to me. Dark brown, light brown, green, yellow, black, mottled, striped. Some with bodies as thick as my neck, others the width of my finger.

They wound around my limbs and I couldn't have moved even if I wanted to.

In front of me stood a woman. She wore a ruffled Cretan gown, just as she had in the image the old woman showed me. There were no snakes wound around her limbs. In fact, a circle surrounded her in which no snake entered.

"You have something I want," she said, and her voice held the sibilance of her snakes.

I could only stare, too scared to even so much as open my mouth. What if a snake slithered in? Would it slide right down my throat and into my belly?

"You need only hand it to me," she said. "And my children will leave you alone."

I tried to convey my feelings through my eyes. Confusion. Hope. Fear.

"Where is it?" she asked. "Answer me."

Please, Isis, don't let any snakes come into my mouth.

"I don't know what you want," I said.

"Give it to me and my children will retreat."

"I would gladly if I knew what you wanted."

"You know. Do not pretend you don't."

"Honestly, I don't know what you want. Tell me and if it is within my power, I will give it to you."

"I want the amulet."

Did she mean the acacia seed pod I still wore on a cord around my neck? Or the spell bottle I gave to Keeper?

"Which one?"

"You know which one."

"I don't, really. Please tell me."

A snake slithered over my head and down my cheek.

"Give it to me," she demanded. "The amulet."

I suddenly understood.

"You want the Eye of Horus," I said. "I don't have it."

"I know you do. Give it to me."

"I already gave it back to Osiris."

She studied me as if trying to determine whether I told the truth.

"You had better get it back then if you want to leave this place," she said.

"I cannot. I have already used it. It can only be used once by a person and never again. He has no reason to give it back since he knows I cannot use it again."

"Unless you give me the amulet, you won't be leaving here and you won't see your friends again."

"If you hurt them, I won't help you."

She raised one eyebrow.

"It didn't sound like you intended to. They are irrelevant anyway. Their only purpose was to see you here safely. Their fates do not matter past that."

"They matter to me, and they matter to themselves."

"Then get the amulet and I will have no reason to harm them."

"Remove your snakes from my body. I can do nothing to help you while they are all over me."

She made a slight hissing sound, as if sucking in air through her teeth. The snakes made their way down my body and away from me. They slithered along the floor or the walls or joined the ones that circled the woman.

She cocked her head and waited.

My limbs were light after the weight of the snakes. I raised shaky hands to inspect them. They hadn't bitten me. She was only trying to scare me. She didn't want to hurt me.

"I have something else I can give you." I pulled the acacia seed pod out from under my gown. "This is a powerful amulet. The healer who gave it to me said it would protect me. I will give you this if you let me leave."

"That is not the amulet I seek."

"But it is the only one I have. I cannot give you what I do not have."

"Go get the one I want."

"I already told you. I gave it to Osiris."

"Then find Osiris and get it from him."

"I cannot. I have already left his Hall once. A living being cannot leave a second time."

I held my breath, wondering if she would recognise my lie. Or maybe it wasn't a lie. I had no way of knowing.

"Then find a way to meet him away from his Hall," she said.

"How? He is a god. I can no more summon a god than I can become one myself."

What was she? A goddess or merely a mortal using some strange connection with snakes? Surely if she had any power other than over her snakes, she would have used it by now. Perhaps she had once been a guardian, but had lost her way, or perhaps she hadn't been able to finish her training. Was this what my daughter would become if Intef stayed and she couldn't learn what she needed to? Would she become some half-mad creature like this? Maybe the old woman's vision of the snake woman was a warning of the danger my daughter would be in if she didn't complete her training.

"I cannot give you what you seek," I said. "And I need to leave this place. So you can either take what I have offered or you can get out of my way."

Her jaw dropped. She had not expected me to stand up to her.

"How dare you?" she screamed. At another hiss, her snakes slithered towards me and wound around me again. "You will go get the amulet."

Maybe her connection with the snakes meant they were precious to her. If I injured one, would she feel its pain? I took a deep breath and steadied myself.

"Get your snakes off me or I will hurt them."

She stretched herself up taller and hissed. More snakes slithered towards me. One large creature, its body as wide as my wrist, wound around my chest. I could hardly breathe. But none of them bit me. I had angered her and yet they didn't bite. Perhaps she had limited control over them.

I unwrapped a small snake from my wrist and held it up high.

"This is your last chance," I said. "Get them off me."

"Do not dare."

I threw the snake down as hard as I could. It landed on a writhing pile and disappeared from my view.

"No," she cried. "Do not harm them."

I untangled another snake from my arm and flung it at a patch of wall that was momentarily clear. It hit the rock and bounced to the ground, where it lay unmoving.

The woman wailed.

One snake at a time, I peeled them off me and flung them away as hard as I could. The snakes seemed confused, unable to interpret the messages from their mistress or whatever she was, or perhaps unwilling to comply. At last she hissed at them and they retreated, withdrawing behind her. Her face was full of fury and her voice trembled.

"You will pay for that."

Yet if she had any other power, she would have already used it.

"I told you to get them off me." I pulled the acacia seed necklace over my head and flung it at her. "Here, take it. This is the only amulet I can give you. Take it and be gone."

It fell at her feet, and for a moment, she only looked at it. She stooped to snatch it up, then turned and fled. With her went her snakes.

The snake woman departed in such a hurry that she left behind her lamp. Thankful for the light, I held it high while I checked for any last snakes, but they were all gone, except for a few broken bodies. I wondered she hadn't taken those with her, too.

I had forgotten my shadow until I saw it sitting against the wall with its legs drawn up to its chest.

"Shadow?" I approached tentatively. "Shadow, are you well?"

It turned its head away from me. An image from a dream flashed through my mind: myself sitting cross-legged in front of my shadow. Perhaps this was the moment in which that was supposed to occur. I sat down and tried to find the right words.

"Were the snakes on you too?" I asked. "I suppose they were. Snakes have shadows, just as all things do."

It raised its arm to show me the shadow of a snake wrapped around its wrist.

"Oh no."

But my shadow seemed unconcerned. It stroked the snake a little, then leaned forward and wrapped its arms around its legs. So one snake had lost its shadow and my shadow had gained a pet, or a friend.

"Will you join with me again?" I asked.

My shadow turned its face away from me.

"Shadow, I need to find my friends, and I cannot leave you here. Please come with me, even if you won't join me."

I couldn't leave this place if my shadow wouldn't rejoin me, but neither could it. I had to trust it wanted to stay here no more than I did.

"Shadow, I am leaving now and I am taking the lamp with me. Please come."

I took a few steps and waited, praying it would follow. It stayed leaning against the wall, but just as I was about to give up hope, it rose.

"Thank you, Shadow."

It gestured towards me, a movement that seemed to indicate it did this for its own reasons and was nothing to do with me.

"That is fine. As long as you come, it doesn't matter why."

I held the lamp higher. Together, my shadow and I walked through the tunnel.

TWENTY-SEVEN

I didn't speak as we walked. I had already said everything I could think of to convince my shadow to rejoin me. There was nothing left to say. Then my foot landed with a splash.

It was only a small puddle, but where did the water come from? In the chaos caused by the snake woman, I had forgotten my fear of tunnels, but it crashed over me now. The earth, the palace foundations. The weight above me must be immense, and the area was unstable. It would not take much to make this whole place tumble down. If water had found its way in, then the tunnels were indeed precarious. I had to get out of here.

"Come on, Shadow," I said. "We need to hurry."

I splashed through another puddle. Then water was everywhere. It covered the entire tunnel floor, only about a finger width in depth, but even as I watched, the water level rose. In moments it was a palm high. Then it was halfway up my calves and up to my shadow's waist.

"Shadow? Are you well?"

Could my shadow drown? What would happen to me if it did?

The memory of the time I drowned flashed through my mind. How did I ever forget such a thing? The ship was wrecked in a storm and I sank deep down into the water. I remembered holding my breath for as long as I could. My lungs had burned and I longed to breathe. I didn't have a clear memory of my thoughts, only impressions of sorrow and regret. I remembered the moment I couldn't hold my breath any longer and the water rushed into my lungs. No, I couldn't drown again.

"Shadow, where are you?"

The water was up to my knees. My thoughts were tangled. I needed to move faster. I needed to get out.

The water now came to my shadow's elbows.

"Shadow."

I reached for it. A pointless attempt since I couldn't touch it.

"Shadow, we don't have much time. Join me before it is too late."

My shadow shook its head and ploughed on.

The water was mid-thigh now for me and mid-chest to my shadow. Could we outrun it before my shadow drowned?

My soaked skirts tangled around my legs until I could barely move. With the lamp, I had only one hand with which to try to free myself, and I couldn't do it.

The water ebbed and flowed, drifting this way, then back that way. It was up to my hips now. My skirts were so tangled that I gave up trying to walk. I wasn't willing to forgo my only light source to untangle them.

"Shadow, where are you?"

But the water was too deep and I could no longer see my shadow.

The water rose over my belly and then my chest. I held the lamp higher, seeking to protect its flame. I couldn't survive this in the dark.

My thoughts were a muddled mix of terror and panic. Half thoughts, phrases, should haves. I had only one coherent thought: that this water was impossible. The labyrinth of tunnels was so vast that it wasn't possible for them to flood so fast, no matter where the water came from.

Be careful of the jackal. He is a trickster.

Was this another of Anubis's tricks? It didn't feel like a trick. The water was up to my shoulders. Now my neck. It was icy and I shivered, hardly able to hold the lamp above the water, and I feared my trembling fingers would drop it.

Don't let me drown. Not again.

There must be a way out of this, if I could calm myself enough to think. I needed something to hold on to, a way of keeping my head above the water. But the rocky walls were smooth and the roof intact.

I couldn't drown again. I wouldn't.

A thought came to my mind. It was audacious, but it might work.

I took a deep breath.

"Guardian of the Path," I cried.

TWENTY-EIGHT

I t was only after I called that I realised my mistake. My daughter was too small, and the water was too deep. Could a goddess-in-training drown?

A figure appeared ahead of me at the very edge of the lamp's reach. She moved towards me and the water didn't cover her as I had expected. Perhaps she was standing on something, or perhaps she somehow floated on the water.

"Can you help me?" I asked.

"He would have stayed if you had not come," she said.

I stammered, trying to find a suitable response.

"This place is killing him," I said. "I can see it. He looks different. Wrong. He cannot stay here, even to be with you."

"I cannot complete my training with him here."

Her voice was placid and I couldn't tell what she was thinking. Perhaps her comment had been an observation rather than a recrimination.

"I will make sure he gets home," I said. "But I cannot if I drown here."

"You would not have drowned."

"The water rose so quickly."

"Did you think it was real?" She tipped her head to the side as she studied me. "Surely you knew?"

"Knew what?"

"About the trials. I thought mortals were aware they would face trials in the underworld."

"We didn't last time."

I waited, but she said nothing further. The water swirled around me. It rose more slowly now. It was almost up to my chin.

"How many trials are there?" I asked.

"As many as needed."

"Are my friends safe? Do they face the same trials?"

She shrugged. I couldn't tell whether she didn't know, or she simply didn't intend to tell me. Perhaps she wasn't permitted to.

"Was it you who warned me about Anubis? That he was a trickster?"

"I suppose it might have been."

"Why?"

"It is my job to see that mortals return safely to their world. His games are a distraction. They will delay you, yes, but if you become too absorbed with them, you might never find your way out."

"Why is Anubis trying to trick me?"

"It is just what he does. He toys with you."

"Is the water another of his tricks?" I asked.

"Trick. Trial. They are not so different from each other."

"How do I get out of the tunnels?"

"The same way you entered."

"I need to find my friends. We have to get back to the mortal world."

"You must find your way out of this trial first."

"But how?"

The water was over my chin. I stretched my neck, holding my head as high as I could, but I wouldn't be able to talk for much longer. I was almost out of time.

"You must remember this is merely a trial. This is not your world and the rules are not the same."

When I opened my mouth to speak, the water poured in. I closed my mouth, swallowed the water. I could say nothing further. I could only stare at her and hope she would understand that I begged for her help.

"It is just a trial. When you find him, tell him…" Her composure flickered and once again I glimpsed her distress. "Tell him I will remember him. And his stories."

Then she was gone.

She said this wasn't real. The currents shifted around me, sometimes bringing a patch of warmer water to brush against my body.

The water was over my mouth. It would be over my nose in moments.

It isn't real. But I shivered and my hair was floating.

It isn't real. But the water was cold and my limbs were light.

The water reached my nose. I held my breath.

It isn't real. But there was no way out.

My lungs hurt. I needed to breathe.

Then I realised. If the water wasn't real, there was no reason to hold my breath. Anubis didn't want to kill me. He already had his chance to give my heart to Ammut. Trick or trial? Did it matter?

I would drown if I was wrong.

I had to believe I wasn't. Perhaps that was the key. Believe the water wasn't real and let myself breathe.

It isn't real.

I opened my mouth and gulped in air.

The water was gone. The tunnels were dry, as was I.

"Thank you, daughter," I whispered.

Perhaps she could hear me, perhaps she wouldn't.

My shadow stood behind me, its shoulders hunched. It didn't need speech to convey its misery.

"Shadow," I gasped, hardly able to breathe. "Are you well?"

It turned its back on me.

I spent a few moments catching my breath.

"I wasn't sure you would come back."

It didn't turn towards me, but its head tilted. It was listening.

"I am so sorry you endured that because of me. I am sorry I didn't realise the water wasn't real sooner."

A slight shrug.

"Shadow, we are stronger together. When we are separated, there is a part of me missing. It is like one of my limbs is gone, or a lung. Some crucial part I cannot live without."

My shadow turned to face me.

"Do you feel it, too?" I whispered. "You feel our separation?"

It nodded.

"Then come back to me. We need to be together to get out of here. I cannot stay in the underworld and I cannot leave without you."

My shadow rubbed its belly.

"I know. Our babes have to stay here. They were born in this place and they cannot leave. They are training to be guardians and they will be together."

It hung its head.

"It makes me sad, too. I think you are the only one who can understand. We will not see our babes grow up. It is a strange place, true, but I think they are already more other than human. They don't belong in the mortal world. They must stay here."

My shadow nodded and placed one hand over its heart.

"It breaks my heart, too, but it is her life, not mine. I have no right to force her to leave the only home she has ever known."

My shadow raised its head and drew back its shoulders.

"Should we go find our friends? Find Intef and your mate?"

It studied me for a long moment, then pointed towards me.

I hesitated. What did it want?

It turned over its hand, palm up. A question.

"I will do better this time. I promised I would talk to you, that I wouldn't forget you, but I didn't do a very good job of it. I didn't try hard enough to remember, maybe because I never thought there would be any consequences if I didn't. I am sorry about that. More sorry than you can know. I have broken a lot of promises and I regret them all. I will work on being a better person and I won't forget my promises anymore. I nearly failed my judgement because of how I treated you. I swear I will not forget you this time."

My shadow considered me for a long moment before it reached towards me. I held out my hand and when our fingers met, I felt the familiar popping and my shadow was back in its usual place, attached to my soles and stretched along the tunnel floor.

"Thank you, Shadow. I promise you will not be sorry you trusted me."

My shadow made no response, but I felt a sense of peace at knowing we were joined again and that I would do better. It would be up to me to remember my shadow was its own being. One day I would face the judges again and I doubted they would accept my forgetting a second time.

TWENTY-NINE

I took random turns as we had before, but Anubis — if it was he who controlled the tunnels — didn't seem inclined to let me find either my friends or the way out. The lamp flickered, likely running low on oil, and I walked faster. I couldn't bear to be here in the dark.

"It is all right, Shadow," I said. "We will find the way out. We just need to trust."

But the lamp dimmed, and soon it went out altogether. I set it on the floor and went back to making my way with one hand on the wall and one hand out in front.

A footstep whispered against the rocky ground.

My heart beat so loudly that surely the beast could hear it.

I opened my mouth to scream, but my throat was too dry and I could make only a strangled gasp.

"Who is there?" someone asked.

Light flared as a lamp was lit.

It was Renni.

"Samun, thank the gods. Are you well?"

I burst into tears.

"It is all right," he said. "I am sure the others will be along soon."

Then Sabu stood with us.

Mahu appeared.

Behenu.

Istnofret.

She came to me and wrapped her arms around me. We didn't speak, just held each other close.

"I am sorry," I whispered to her.

She only nodded and sniffled.

Behenu came to put her arms around both of us.

Then Tuta appeared.

"Tuta!" Behenu said. She went to him and for a moment, I thought she would hug him. But then her arms dropped and she stepped back. "I was worried about you."

"I wasn't sure we would see you again, man," Renni said, slapping Tuta on the back.

Tuta looked a little dazed and could only shake his head.

Only Intef was missing.

We waited.

"Do you think…" Behenu started, but her voice trailed away.

"Hush," Istnofret said. "He will be along sooner or later. We just need to wait."

"Maybe he won't," I said. "Maybe…"

I couldn't make myself say it, that maybe the judges had deemed him unworthy and Ammut had eaten his heart. He would not return to us if that was the case. Nor would he have any chance at an afterlife. Once Ammut ate your heart, there was nothing but oblivion.

"Samun." Istnofret spoke hesitantly. "Did you face judgement?"

"I did. You too?"

She nodded. I glanced at the others and they all nodded.

"What… how…" I didn't know what to ask. They must have all passed the weighing of the heart or they wouldn't be here. I wasn't sure it was even appropriate to ask what happened.

"Anubis took my heart right out of my chest," Renni said. "I thought I was going to die."

"My heart was heavier than the Feather at first," Sabu said. "I had to justify some things I did in Pharaoh's service."

"Me too," Renni said.

"I thought for sure I would not get out of there," Mahu said. "All the lies I've told, things I've stolen when I was too sick to work. I suppose I never thought I would have to account for them."

"You did what you needed to survive," Renni said. "And they must have realised that."

"I had to account for the man I killed," Istnofret said, her voice very quiet. "The judges considered that for a long time. It didn't seem to be enough that I killed him to save myself."

"As did I," Renni said. "The man in the tunnels below Hattusa, amongst other things. I think the only thing that saved me was that it was an accident. I didn't mean to kill him."

"You have paid for his death over and over," Istnofret said. "The guilt you felt must have swayed them."

Renni shrugged. "They seemed more concerned about what I did than how I felt afterwards."

"What did they say, Ist?" I asked. "About the man you killed?"

She stared down at her hands for a while and I thought she wouldn't answer. Perhaps I shouldn't have asked.

"You told me once that it changes a person to kill a man," she said. "I did what I needed to do and I've never even felt guilty about it. Not the way Renni did about the man in the tunnels. I did what I had to, and it was his own fault, really. I'm not sure it changed me like you said it would, and I've felt more guilt about that than about killing him. The judges asked several questions about it and my heart in the scale sank even lower with each one. I was sure that one act would be what doomed me."

"But it didn't," I said. "They wouldn't have let you go if they didn't think you had justified yourself."

She shrugged and didn't reply.

"What about you, Behenu?" Renni asked.

"My heart was the same weight as the Feather," Behenu said. "I suppose I have not done anything of particular importance. They asked me about Horemheb and how I thought about trying to kill him so I could escape. But since I didn't do it, I am not sure it had much impact on my judgement. They mostly focused on how I didn't want the life my father intended for me. The little ways I used to rebel against him."

"So what made the difference?" he asked. "There must have been something you said that made your heart lighter?"

"I told them I would like the chance to go home," she said. "Back to Syria so I can talk to my father. I will tell him I don't want that life. See if we can find a way to agree. They seemed satisfied with that."

"What about you, Tuta?" I asked. "What happened when you fell into the tunnels?"

"I fell through the roof of the tunnels, yes," Tuta said. "But when I landed, it was in a strange cavern that didn't seem to have any exits. I started walking, meaning to search the perimeter and see if there might be a way out, and discovered the walls to be some kind of illusion."

"We were there too," Renni said. "But it must have been after you. We entered through an enormous building with all different doors. We fell down into that cavern."

"I was walking along, then suddenly I found myself in Osiris's Hall," Tuta said. "Anubis took my heart out of my chest. I could feel it beating even as he placed it on the scales. It sank, but not as far as I might have expected. I had to account for various things I have done, like the rest of you. They particularly wanted to hear about Khay and what I thought might have happened if I hadn't killed him. Eventually my heart rose higher than the Feather and they let me leave. I started walking, then suddenly I was here with all of you."

"I was very worried about you," Behenu said. "We didn't know whether you had survived the fall. I hated leaving you there."

"I would not have expected anyone to search for me," Tuta said. "From what you all said about this place, I figured you would know I hadn't fallen into the tunnels and merely waited for you to find me. I knew you would know I was somewhere else."

"I wonder why, though," Istnofret said. "Why did they separate you from us?"

Tuta shrugged. "Perhaps an opportunity arose when I fell. Maybe it was part of a game and didn't have any particular significance."

"I wonder if you might have been useful in some way," Renni said. "Perhaps with you we would have found our way through the tunnels faster or we would have found Anubis's gates sooner. By separating us, maybe it made the tests, or whatever they were, last longer."

"I suppose we will never know," Sabu said. "I am just pleased to have you back with us."

Then Intef appeared. He was pale and barely seemed able to stand. Renni grabbed him by the arms. They looked at each other for a long moment. Intef nodded, and Renni stepped back.

"Intef."

My voice was tiny. After everything I had done, he wouldn't want anything to do with me. If he hated me for giving our daughter to Osiris, he would hate me even more for taking him away from her. One day I would tell him I saw Meketaten again. How she helped me. I would give him her message. Just not today. The pain of losing her again was too raw.

"You took your time," Renni said before I could say anything else.

Intef looked at him a little blankly. At last he shook his head as if to rid himself of unwanted thoughts.

"I was judged," he said.

"We all were," Renni said.

"Anubis. He took my heart right out of my chest. I had to account for all the things I have done. The people I have killed, the lies I have told." Intef paused and shot me a look. "The resentment I have felt."

I opened my mouth, but closed it again. There were things I needed to tell him, but this wasn't the right moment.

"They seemed less concerned with what I had done or what I thought and more with *why*," he said. "I always knew I would have a lot to account for in my judgement, but I expected the judges to focus on my actions, not my reasons."

"I suppose there is a big difference between killing a man because you want to and killing him because you are protecting someone you love," Behenu said. "You, of all people, Intef, have not done things you cannot justify."

"I think I have," he said.

"Let's get out of here," Sabu said, before Intef could say anything more. "I am longing for fresh air."

"Samun, take this lamp." Renni held it out to me. "I want to keep my hands free."

"I have a feeling we will be able to find our way out now," Istnofret said. "Surely we have endured all the tests and trials that might be required and there is nothing else left."

I had to tell them. Now, before we went any further. It was too late for anyone to choose not to go, but they should know we would be hunted before we left this place. As I opened my mouth, a noise came from behind me. The scuff of a claw against rock. Perhaps a soft growl. Nobody else seemed to notice as they chatted and adjusted their packs.

"Maybe we should have something to eat before we start walking," Behenu said. "There is still some—"

She stopped as a growl echoed through the tunnel.

"What... what is that?" Istnofret whispered.

"It is the beast." Behenu's face was stricken. "The one the priests told us about."

"We do not know that," Renni said. "We should all keep calm—"

The growl sounded again, closer this time.

Someone grabbed my shoulder and pushed me, hard.

"Back against the wall," Tuta said. "Get behind us."

Istnofret, Behenu and I huddled together against the wall, with the five men in a tight line in front of us, their daggers already in their hands. I set the lamp down, almost knocking it over, and fumbled my dagger out of my pouch. My hands shook and it landed on the rocky floor with a clang. Renni shot me a look.

"Sorry, sorry," I whispered, fumbling for the dagger. I didn't seem able to see properly, but at last my fingers found it.

"Here it comes," Tuta said.

They would protect us.

But as we waited for the beast to come around the corner, my fear turned to rage. Was this another of Anubis's tricks, or merely a resident of the tunnels? Regardless, why should we women cower behind the men? Why should they risk their lives to save us? We all had daggers. We could all fight. On trembling legs, I stepped forward to stand beside Mahu. He gave me a bewildered look.

There was no time to explain.

I had only heard the beast in my dreams and my imagination had failed to create a creature half as terrifying. I had pictured something like Ammut, which was a mix of crocodile and lion and hippopotamus, for she was the most fearsome creature I knew of.

This beast looked nothing like Ammut, though. Its head was like a bull, with fearsome horns and eyes clouded with rage. Beneath the bull's head, its form was that of a man, although the hands and feet ended in claws rather than fingers. It was mostly naked, although the tattered remnants of something that might once have been a shirt hung from its shoulders. When the beast saw us, it tipped back its head and roared, showing a mouthful of yellowed teeth.

"Isis, protect us," Istnofret murmured.

I hadn't realised she had come forward to stand beside me. Behenu, too. We would all fight the beast.

"Stay back," Renni called. "If you can understand me, stay where you are. We have no wish to hurt you, but we will defend ourselves."

The beast looked right at him and roared. Did it understand his words or did it know only that he threatened it?

We waited.

The beast roared again. It seemed confused. Perhaps it was not accustomed to people doing anything other than running away? At last it stalked towards us, placing each clawed foot slowly, deliberately. It didn't seem to be in a hurry. Was it trying to give us time to flee?

"Shouldn't we be running?" Istnofret whispered.

When it was no more than the length of a man away from us, the beast stopped. Its beady gaze seemed to linger on me and it started to step forward again.

"No."

Intef moved to stand in front of me.

"You will not have her."

The beast looked him right in the eyes and roared.

"If you take another step, I will attack," Intef said.

Very deliberately, the beast stepped forward.

Intef lunged with his dagger, but the beast moved, dancing back out of his reach. Then Renni was beside Intef.

The beast looked from one to the other as it swiped at them.

Renni cried out as its claws caught him on the shoulder.

Tuta, Sabu and Mahu advanced, and the five of them surrounded the beast.

I clutched my dagger with sweaty fingers. They knew what they were doing. I would be nothing but a distraction if I tried to help. But if the beast broke through, I would be ready.

The beast howled, a sound of pain this time. Someone's dagger had found its mark. It stumbled backwards, almost tripping over Mahu and sending him flying to the ground. The beast raised one claw to touch the blood oozing from its chest. It was not a mortal wound, nor even a particularly deep one, just a shallow cut through muscle. Still, the beast seemed bewildered at its injury.

"Run," Intef said.

THIRTY

We fled. There was no time to grab our packs, but I did snatch up the lamp. I was so intent on keeping hold of it, I didn't even notice when I dropped my dagger. I only realised at some point that I no longer held it.

Stay calm, stay calm, I thought, but it didn't help. *Isis, protect us.* This was it. The scene from my dream. Someone would die within the next few moments. It would be either me or one of the others.

Somebody jostled me as they ran past. My heart beat so loudly that I couldn't hear whether the beast still followed us. Then it roared. I could hear that much.

I couldn't breathe. A panicked moan escaped my lips. Somewhere up ahead, the tunnel was lighter. We took the turn that led towards the light, but there was just more tunnel.

"Faster," someone said, their voice so choked I couldn't tell who it was. "It is catching up."

My legs shook so badly that surely they wouldn't hold me much longer. *Don't fall down. The beast will get you.*

The lamp light bounced around, but at least we had light.

Right in front of me was Istnofret. She held her skirts high as she ran. I glimpsed Tuta in front of her with Behenu beside him. Her gait hitched as she ran — the wound in her thigh still made her limp. Renni glanced back.

"Keep up, Mahu," he called.

More light up ahead. But more tunnel when we turned towards it.

Beside me was Sabu, his face white with terror. I stumbled and he grabbed my arm, somehow keeping me on my feet. Where was Intef? I couldn't see him. Isis, please don't let him be the one who dies.

A growl came from right behind us. The beast had caught up.

"Go," Sabu cried. He got behind me, almost tripping me as he did. He shoved me, urging me on faster. I wanted to tell him he should stay beside me, not fall behind. But I was out of breath and I needed all my energy to keep pumping my legs and I said nothing.

Another turn towards the light. More tunnel.

Someone screamed, and there was a meaty thud as they fell.

"Don't stop," Intef called.

Somebody grabbed my hand and pulled me along with them.

Another scream

Bones crunched.

"Keep running."

Light ahead. Another turn. Then we rounded a bend and came to the place where the roof had collapsed in.

"Go, go," Renni called. He stopped beside the rock pile and waved us forward. "Up. Quickly."

I scrambled up the rocks, putting my foot right through my skirt in my haste. I dropped the lamp and it rolled away with a clatter.

"Leave it," came Intef's voice from behind me. "Just go."

Then I was out of the tunnel. It was night, and the air was fresh and the moon was shining. I fell as I reached the surface, then tripped over my torn skirt. On hands and knees, I scrambled over the rubble.

"Not that way." Tuta's voice.

Something grabbed my foot.

I kicked and screamed.

"You're going the wrong way. You have to go this way."

Then Intef was there, grabbing me by the arms. "Up. Come on."

He led me across the rubble and over to the grass.

Behenu already stood there, her face white.

Right behind me was Istnofret with Tuta, then Sabu.

Renni was the last to cross.

Mahu didn't come.

"Run," Renni said.

I didn't think my legs could run anymore, but somehow I did.

"Stop," Istnofret gasped at last. "I cannot run anymore."

My lungs heaved, and I couldn't catch my breath. I leaned over, hands on my knees.

"Far enough?" Tuta asked.

"I think so," Intef said. "There is no sign of pursuit."

"Probably because it is still eating Mahu." Behenu's voice trembled so much I could barely understand her.

"Poor Mahu," Istnofret said. "Do you think…"

"No chance, love," Renni said. "I saw enough to be certain."

Istnofret covered her face with her hands.

"Why did he even come with us?" I asked. "He shouldn't have."

"He couldn't keep up," Renni said. "I knew he wasn't strong enough. He offered to watch our packs, but I told him to come."

"He won't have an afterlife," Istnofret whispered. "We have to go back for him."

"The beast was eating him, love." Renni's voice was gentle but firm. "Even if we could sneak back in and avoid the beast's notice while we retrieve him, there's part of him already gone and we won't get that back. I will not risk our lives to retrieve just part of a man."

"He is your friend." Istnofret half-heartedly beat him with her fists. "You cannot leave him there."

"It is all right." Renni wrapped his arms around her. "Cry, love. Let it out. He was a good man and we will miss him."

"It isn't fair." She sobbed into his chest.

I wrapped my arms around myself and tried to pretend I wasn't crying. I didn't dare look at Intef in case he thought I expected him to comfort me, as Renni did Istnofret. He might not hate me anymore, but I wasn't sure he still loved me. I let myself collapse down onto the grass and wrapped my arms around my knees while I cried.

When my tears finally stopped, Istnofret and Renni were sitting not far from me, she leaning against his shoulder and he with an arm around her. Behenu and Tuta sat close together, not quite touching. Sabu lay stretched out on the grass, staring up at the stars. Intef stood some distance away, looking towards the ruins. Keeping watch for any sign of the beast, I assumed.

"Maybe we should move on," Renni said at last.

"Did anyone else see the light in the tunnels?" Sabu asked.

"I thought it would lead us out," Renni said. "I kept taking the turn I thought took us towards the light, but never seemed to find it."

"It was Meketaten," Intef said. "She guided us through the dark."

"How do you know?" I asked.

I wanted to believe our daughter had helped us escape, but like Renni, I saw nothing other than light we couldn't find.

Intef shrugged. "I just know. Her job is to help those who shouldn't be here to leave. If someone helped us to find the right path down there, it was her."

I sent up a silent prayer of thanks. Would my daughter hear me pray to her? She was almost a goddess, after all.

We didn't speak again as we returned to where we had left the rest of our things with the old man to guard over them. I was relieved to see the cart was still there, for we had left our packs behind when we ran from the beast. The old man was there, too, curled up on the grass and sound asleep. Renni woke him and gestured for him to return to his home. He offered the man a loaf of bread, which he took with many bows of thanks. Surely no more than a single night had passed here or the old man would have already left.

"Some of our gems were in the packs we left behind," Istnofret said. "I still have mine, but the ones Renni carried were in his pack."

"Mine are in my pouch and I still have it," Behenu said.

I fumbled at my waist, relieved to find my pouch was where it should be.

"Me too," I said.

"We will have enough to live on," Renni said. "Enough that we need never worry about working again. The ones we left behind can stay there."

"But that is a fortune," Istnofret said. "Several fortunes. What if we need them later?"

"Then we will know where to find them," Renni said. "Surely, love, you aren't suggesting we risk our lives to go back down into the tunnels to retrieve the gems?"

Istnofret's face showed her conflict.

"Let's get away from here for now," Renni said. "Later, once we are all calmer, we can think this through and decide what to do. We can come back if we decide we need to retrieve the gems. They are safe enough where they are for now."

"We need somewhere to sleep," Behenu said. "Solid walls. I don't think I can camp outside tonight."

"We will find a house," Tuta said. "Don't worry. You are safe."

He reached over to grasp her hand briefly, then looked away, as if fearing he had said too much.

THIRTY-ONE

I t was dawn by the time we reached Katsamba and we quickly secured accommodation. Although the day was warm, we stayed inside with the door locked. Behenu checked Renni's shoulder where the beast had slashed at him and said the wound wasn't very deep. We had plenty of supplies, but I had little appetite. When I tried to eat, it reminded me of the sound of the beast tearing Mahu apart.

As night fell, we closed the shutters and lit a lamp. I wrapped myself in a blanket, even though it was really too warm. My insides were cold and perhaps I would never be warm again. I lay with my back against the wall. Istnofret was beside me with Renni on her other side. At the other end of the chamber were Behenu, Tuta and Sabu. Intef stood at the window, having offered to take the first watch.

Every time I closed my eyes, I saw the beast tearing off Mahu's limbs, even though I had seen no such thing while we were in the tunnels. I kept hearing his cry as the beast pounced, his bones crunching as it attacked. Why had we let him come with us? He, of all of us, was the one least able to outrun the creature. I was bitterly ashamed of the tiny part of me that was relieved it was Mahu and not me or one of my friends. I was still awake when Intef shook Tuta's shoulder to wake him for guard duty.

The other future I saw in the dream in which the beast hunted us had been my own death, but what decision did I make that meant it was Mahu rather than me? The only thing I could think of was the fact that I hadn't told them we would be hunted. Would that have made the difference? Would knowing about the beast have meant they would all be more prepared and I would be the one to die? Perhaps we wouldn't have let Mahu come with us, or perhaps he would have chosen to stay with our packs.

Sometime before Tuta's watch ended, I must have fallen asleep, for I found myself standing in front of Suppiluliumas. Or at least I assumed it was him. It was the same man I had seen once before in a dream. He looked past me and when I turned to see what he was looking at, Ay stood there. His hands were bound and his face was furious.

The dream shifted, and I found myself in a setting I had seen before. Two armies fought, Egyptian against Hittite. Beside me, Suppiluliumas smiled.

"Now I will lay waste to your entire country," he said. "Never again will Egypt dare to kill a son of the Hittites."

THIRTY-TWO

"I am going home," Behenu announced as we broke our fast the following day. "Back to Syria."

"Oh, Behenu." Istnofret's voice was mournful. "We had hoped you might stay here."

"I wish I could, but I told the judges I would talk to my father. Perhaps if I tell him the life he wants for me is not the path I want, he will allow me to choose for myself."

"And if he doesn't?" I asked.

Behenu fiddled with a half-eaten fig, peeling away a little of the skin.

"Then I must do what I was raised to. There are obligations on me and they cannot be passed to someone else if I don't want them. Only one with the ability can fulfil them. The gods gave me that ability, so if my father will not release me, I must live the life they intended for me."

"I will come with you if I may," Tuta said.

She barely startled. It seemed she was growing accustomed to his attentions.

"I would see you safely there," he said. "You may have need of a guard on the journey."

Behenu blushed a little.

"I would welcome your company," she said, staring down at the fig in her hand.

"We intend to stay here," Renni said. "Ist and I. Having seen this place again, she is more determined than ever to live here."

"Even after the beast?" I asked.

"We will live somewhere along the coast," Istnofret said. "We will be a long way from the beast there. The people here do not seem to live in fear and Renni says the priests talked only of a beast that roamed the tunnels, not one that terrorised the villages, so I think we will be safe enough. I want a little house where I can see the sea."

I smiled and tried to hide my sadness. I had known the day would come when we all went our separate ways, but I hadn't thought it would be today. But we had done what we came here for and there was no reason for anyone to linger.

"What about you, Sabu?" Renni avoided looking at either Intef or me.

"I suppose I shall go back to Egypt," Sabu said. "It is all I know. I cannot see myself living somewhere else."

"You shall take a couple of gems, of course," I said. "You won't need to work again."

He gave me a grateful smile and dipped his head in acknowledgement. I suddenly realised I knew almost nothing about him. I didn't even know whether he had a wife or a family waiting for him back in Egypt.

"And what of you?" Sabu asked me.

I stared down at my hands while I tried to come up with a convincing lie. Intef and I had once planned to live near Istnofret and Renni. Even yesterday, I might still have considered this, but after my dream, I knew that wasn't possible. Not yet, at any rate. The Hittites were still a threat and I hadn't done what I told Osiris I would. As long as the possibility of war lingered, my quest was incomplete.

I couldn't tell them, though. I didn't want anyone to feel obliged to come with me. They had done enough. It was time for them all to be free to live their own lives.

"I think I will go home," I said. "For now, at least. I would like to find Maia again. Find out how she knew the things she did."

"I said you would keep finding more things to do." Istnofret sounded rather grumpy. "When are you going to live your life? Leave Egypt in the hands of the gods like you said you would."

"I will, but I have questions that need answers first. I want to know where Maia's information came from. How she knew to send me to Bhumi. How she knew Shala would have told her about the Eye."

Istnofret shot Renni a look, but he shook his head.

"No, Ist," he said. "You promised. You swore we would be finished once we retrieved Intef. This is our time now."

Istnofret nodded, but her face revealed her conflicted feelings.

"Renni is right," I said. "You have done your part. Stay here like you said you would. Perhaps I am not the sort of person who will ever settle down. Maybe you are right and I will keep finding one quest after another to chase."

"I cannot live like that, Ist," Renni said quietly. "I want my own home. Children. A job. I want to wake up in my own bed every day."

Istnofret reached for his hand.

"I promised," she said. "We will stay in Crete, and you can be a soldier again. I am feeling rather tired after all our adventures."

"We have had more adventures than most people could even dream of," Renni said. "Think of the stories we will tell our children. They probably won't believe most of them."

She smiled and leaned her head against his shoulder.

"What about you, Intef?" Sabu asked. "Will you stay in Crete too?"

So I wasn't the only one who assumed Intef wanted nothing to do with me. The knowledge made my heart hurt even more.

"I will return to Egypt, of course." Intef sounded surprised. "With Samun."

"What?" I blurted before I could stop myself.

He gave me a hesitant look, seeming confused.

"As long as you want me to, that is," he said. "I know we haven't talked yet, but I assumed..."

His voice trailed away. Renni stood up.

"I think I have some chores to do," he said. "Outside. I will need help."

In moments, the cottage was empty except for Intef and I. He stared at the floor and seemed to avoid looking at me.

"Intef," I said.

He didn't look up.

"Intef, of course I want you to come with me. But I didn't think it was what you wanted anymore."

"Why? My feelings have not changed. Have yours?"

"Of course not. But I thought you hated me."

He finally looked at me, his face a mix of hope and dread.

"I did," he said. "And I had to account for that to the judges. At first I hated you for giving Meketaten to Osiris. But she never could have left the underworld, and when Keeper demanded a living soul, it gave me the chance to be with our daughter. To love her and to teach her. She is a most unusual girl, Samun. Like nobody I have ever met, although I see reflections of you in her."

He wiped away tears and gave me a small smile.

"Then when you came to take me away from her, I hated you all over again. But if Meketaten says there are things she cannot learn with me there, I have to trust she knows better than I what her training will involve. Everything you have done has been for reasons you thought were right. I cannot say I have always agreed with your decisions, but you have never had any selfish or hateful motive. You are just being you, trying to fix the world. And I love you for that."

My chin wobbled, and I desperately tried not to cry. I would tell him Meketaten's message later. I wouldn't be able to hold myself together if I had to do it now.

"I need to tell you something before you decide to come back with me," I said.

"I already know you have some other quest in mind," he said. "You are not a very good liar, Samun, but you can explain it to me later. Let us deal with farewelling our friends before I have to worry about what you plan to do next."

THIRTY-THREE

We made our preparations to leave much faster than I might have hoped. Intef went to find out when the next ship would depart for Egypt and returned with news that we could leave at dawn. He had secured passage for the three of us — me, himself and Sabu. He also procured a new dagger for me. It was a little smaller than my old one and fit my hand better. I tucked it away in my pouch where it would always be ready should I need it.

Renni and Istnofret arranged to continue to hire the cottage while they decided where to live. Renni intended to build a house for them, but Istnofret wanted to find the most perfect location on the island first. Behenu and Tuta would leave for Syria in two days. I didn't know whether any promises had been made between them — they never said, and I didn't think it right to ask — but I noticed Behenu now wore a russet sapphire on a cord around her neck. It was the gem I had given Tuta before we left Egypt.

We ate our last meal together on blankets on the grass as the sun sank beneath a brilliant lavender sunset. I tried to hide my sombre mood, since everyone else seemed joyous. We ate freshly caught fish grilled over coals until it flaked apart. The fish was sweet and tasted of the sea, and it made me homesick for fish from the Great River. Renni had procured a couple of bottles of wine, which everyone else drank with gusto. It was too tart for my taste, and I set my mug aside after a few sips.

The wine reminded me of the bottle we brought for Intef. As if she had read my mind, Behenu appeared at my side with the bottle.

"I thought you might want this," she said.

"Thank you."

I caught Intef's eye and motioned for him to follow me. We went off a little way from the others and sat down. The grass was cool and soft beneath me. Intef sat with a groan and I shot him a worried look. It wasn't like him to give any indication of pain.

"Are you well?" I asked.

"My back aches," he said. "Some days are worse than others. I think my body is still adjusting to the loss of my arm. Things hurt that never used to. I suppose I will get used to it with time."

"I am sorry it still hurts."

I didn't know how else to respond. He no longer held a grudge against me for being the one to decide to cut off his arm, or at least he said he didn't. I still felt guilt about it, even though it was the only way to save his life.

"The others are certainly feeling festive." He gave me a careful look. "You don't seem to feel the same."

"I am sad to be saying goodbye to Istnofret, Behenu and Renni. We have been together so long, the five of us."

"All things pass, and they have their own lives to live, as do we."

It was a subtle reminder of what he wanted. A house of his own, he had said to me at some point. Children. His own vegetable patch, or perhaps it was his own dom palm tree. I couldn't quite remember now. Regardless, he wouldn't follow me forever. Eventually, he would do as Renni had and insist it was time to settle down.

"I brought something for you." I offered him the bottle. "From Memphis."

He held it up to inspect the label and I remembered with a pang that he couldn't read.

"From your brother's vineyard?" he asked.

"I promised myself once I would ensure you got the chance to drink Pharaoh's own wine."

"Why in the name of the gods would you promise such a thing?" He removed the stopper and sniffed the contents. "Ahh, that is good."

"Do you remember when you took me to the festival of Isis?"

"Of course I do. That was the night you first kissed me."

"We drank wine. I thought it was horrible, but you said it was what you were used to. I promised myself then that one day I would make sure you drank from Pharaoh's vineyard."

Intef raised the bottle and took a swig.

"Oh yes, that is a fine wine," he said.

He offered it back to me.

"I should have brought some mugs," I said.

He grinned. "Go on, Samun. Drink from the bottle. Nobody other than me will ever know."

I snatched it from him and took a long drink.

"Tastes like home," I said.

"I am sure there is more where that came from."

"A whole cellar of it. I don't intend to go back to Memphis, though, if that is what you are trying to ask. Intef, I have done terrible things. I took the throne from Ay, but then I…"

My voice trailed away as I realised I didn't know how to tell him about the things I had done while under the Eye's influence. I wasn't even sure I wanted him to know. He would never look at me the same way again.

"Don't tell me tonight." He reached for the bottle. "Leave it for another day. We all have enough to process tonight with saying goodbye to the others and Renni seems to be taking Mahu's loss hard. Once we are out at sea will be soon enough for you to tell me however much you think I need to know."

A cheer from Renni interrupted as I started to reply.

"To Mahu," Renni cried. "May he live for a million years."

The others responded enthusiastically. I waited until the noise died down before I spoke again.

"I am not the same person I used to be, Intef."

"I would not expect you to be. Too much has happened for any of us to be the same as when we first set off on your grand quest."

"I am afraid you will think less of me once you hear it all."

"You forget I know you, Samun." He offered me the bottle again. "I have seen the darkness in you as well as the greatness. It doesn't scare me."

"Will you tell me about Meketaten?"

He sighed and fiddled with the label on the bottle.

"I will, but not today. I have not quite come to terms with losing her yet. I know it is better for her this way, but I cannot help thinking it is not best for me."

"I understand."

Now was not the time to tell him how I envied his time with her.

"So tomorrow we will be at sea yet again." Intef's fingers brushed mine as he passed me the bottle. "Just like old times."

"Except it will be just you and me. And Sabu."

"We have spent so much time at sea over the last couple of years that I feel quite at home out there now."

"I don't think I will ever feel comfortable on the water."

The call of the waves. The memory of sinking down into deep water before I drowned.

"Perhaps this will be the last time you need to sail," he said. "Once we do whatever this last thing is, we can settle in Egypt."

"I might never see Istnofret again."

This could be farewell forever. If I never sailed again, I probably wouldn't ever see her. Once Istnofret and Renni had a brood of children, they would be unlikely to uproot them to sail all the way to Egypt just to see an old friend. And if Intef and I had more children of our own, we likely wouldn't travel either.

Not that I knew whether he wanted another babe. Perhaps the loss of two was heartbreak enough. I couldn't ask what he thought, because he would ask how I felt, and I didn't have an answer for that yet.

"Do you want the last drop?" he asked.

"You finish it."

He drained the bottle, then set it aside and lay back on the grass to stare up at the stars.

"Lie with me," he said.

I lay down beside him. The stars were brilliant tonight, an uncountable sea spread across the sky.

"Do you still wonder which ones are your brother and your father?" he asked.

"If I see the first stars come out at dusk, I think that is them. I cannot find them when there are so many."

"It is a beautiful thought, that your loved ones are up there looking down on you."

"Not all my loved ones."

I rolled onto my side to face him and he turned his head to study me.

"You are right," he said. "You are changed."

"For better or worse?" I held my breath as I waited for his answer.

"You seem freer. Less cautious. You hold yourself apart from everyone else a little less."

He rolled over to face me. His stump was beneath him, and like this, he looked like he was before we took his arm. In the moonlight I couldn't see the greyness of his skin. Perhaps it would fade with time and the further we got from the underworld. He ran one finger down the side of my cheek.

"Even when we were together, I never felt like you saw me. Me, Intef. The man. Not just the guard charged with protecting you. Not just your captain. This is the first time I have ever felt like you really saw me."

He was right, of course. I had spent so long thinking of him as my guard — my guardian — that I had rarely seen him for himself. I hadn't ever looked at him as the man who loved me. He had always been my protector.

"I have had a lot of time to think," I said. "Being separated from you, not knowing whether I would see you again. You have saved me so many times and yet suddenly I had to save myself."

My voice was husky. The moment felt too intimate and my old instinct to run away rose up. I pushed it back down. If I fled now, he would think I hadn't changed at all.

"I wondered whether the day would come when you asked me to prove myself to you," I said. "To prove I loved you."

He barked out a laugh. "I was just a boy when my father told me there could never be anything between you and me, that I would save myself from a lifetime of heartache if I could forget about you, but I couldn't do it."

"It must have been painful for you, to love me all those years and think I would never love you."

"There were days I told myself I should leave. Go somewhere far away where nobody knew your name and where I would never come across any memory of you again. But I couldn't. At least as your captain, I got to see you every day. I resigned myself to that. Told myself it was enough."

"That is why you always took the day shift, isn't it? So you could see me? I thought for a while that perhaps you had a family, or even just someone you spent your nights with."

He laughed. "My men didn't dare complain, but I knew they thought I took the day shifts because they were more interesting than standing by your door all night."

"Did none of them know how you felt?"

"I never spoke of it, but I suppose some might have guessed. Khay probably. Later, maybe Renni. It is hard to conceal such a thing from those you work so closely with."

We were silent for a while. I rolled over to stare up at the stars again. My father and brother were up there. All our pharaohs were there, even Hatshepsut who many now considered a heretic for daring to call herself Pharaoh despite being a woman. When Intef spoke, it was as if he knew I was thinking about pharaohs.

"I don't think I ever told you how proud I was of you the day you claimed the throne."

For a moment, I was confused. I hadn't told him what happened in Memphis. But of course he meant the first time I claimed the throne, just after my brother had gone to the West.

"I didn't get to keep it for very long," I said.

Ay had brought his soldiers and I gave up the throne almost as soon as I took it.

"Do you wonder how different things might have been if you had stood your ground that day?" he asked. "We could have fought. We might have won."

"He had far more men than you did and besides, I already knew how it would end. I saw it in a dream. I watched you die right there on the floor and I couldn't let that happen. Ay had the superior numbers and he would have taken the throne from me whether you fought or not. The difference was that you lived and I knew that was important. I think I loved you then, even if I didn't know it."

"Tell me something, love," he said. "Why did you come to get me? I have puzzled over this and still don't understand. I was the price for you to all pass through the gates, so why would you come back for me?"

"Because I knew you would have come for me. You wouldn't leave me there."

"It has always been me saving you," he said. "I guess I never thought that one day you would be the one to save me."

THIRTY-FOUR

O ur farewells the following morning were briefer than one might expect for folk who have known each other for so long. Perhaps none of us could bear to say goodbye. We would never all be together again, not with Behenu returning to Syria.

"I wish you freedom," I said as I hugged her. "Freedom to be who you want, not who your father wants."

"I have reconciled myself to it," she said. "If he insists, I will do my duty."

"And Tuta? What of him?"

She touched the sapphire at her throat, then pulled her hand away as if only just realising what she did.

"He is a good man," she said. "I am not sure why he has chosen me, but I will let him see me home. I want him to meet my father, to understand my situation there before I make any decisions. Perhaps once he realises what I am, he will change his mind."

"A truth speaker," I said.

She shot me a startled look.

"How do you know?" she asked. "I never told you that."

"Mutnodjmet told me, just before we left Memphis. I don't understand what it means, though."

"It is something like an oracle. Someone you might go to in search of wisdom. "

"Is a truth-speaker born? Or taught?"

"Both. One must be born with the ability, but the truth-speaker is trained from childhood in many things, not just seeing the truth. Healing, divinations, politics. There are many demands, many expectations of a trained truth-speaker."

"Does that have something to do with why you wanted to be my spy?"

She laughed a little.

"I wanted a fate I chose for myself," she said. "Children are tested for the truth at a very young age and once a truth-speaker is found, their life is never their own again. I wanted to make my own choice. I don't think I was a very good spy, though."

I understood the sentiment, perhaps more than she realised. I was born a princess and raised with the expectation of being useful to my pharaoh, of knowing I would give myself over to his whim. But now I was too used to making my own decisions to return to a life where I was controlled. Perhaps Behenu would change her mind once she felt like her freedom was gone. Perhaps she wouldn't.

Behenu was pulled away into other farewells and I watched for a few moments before I realised Istnofret stood beside me. She wrapped her arm around my waist.

"I will miss you, my lady," she said.

"You shouldn't call me that anymore."

Istnofret laughed.

"I just wanted to say it one last time," she said. "I will always think fondly of those days. When it was Sadeh and Charis and me."

"It seems like such a long time ago."

"It was, and yet it wasn't. We are such different people now. I don't know if I could do it again. Be a serving lady. Always at somebody's beck and call."

"I didn't work you too hard." Even so, I felt a pang of guilt. "You had much time for needlework and walking in the gardens and whatever else you wanted."

"Oh, I know. You were the best mistress I could have asked for and I don't for a minute regret those years. But I am not the person I once was."

"None of us are. We couldn't be after all we have seen."

"Who could ever have imagined you and I would travel all the way across the world and even into the underworld? The things we have seen. But I have had enough adventures for now."

"You don't seem as happy to be back here as I thought you would be."

I held my breath, wondering whether I shouldn't have said it.

She gave a heavy sigh.

"I knew from the moment we set foot on Crete again that our time together was almost over," she said. "That this would be the end of our journey. Renni says I should wait until you leave before I grieve for you, but I couldn't stop myself from feeling sorrowful."

Renni came over, and the moment was gone. He didn't speak much, either to me or to Intef. They seemed to do no more than slap each other on the back.

It was easier to say goodbye to Tuta.

"Look after her," I said, with a glance in Behenu's direction.

He blushed a little.

"Istnofret has already given me an earful," he said. "You do not need to say it again."

"It will be difficult for her to return home after all this time."

"She has told me a little about her life there. She didn't say it, but I gather she is important. I am looking forward to seeing Syria. I never expected to travel outside of Egypt."

Intef waved to let me know it was time to leave. We picked up our packs and prepared to go.

"Got your arm?" Renni asked.

Intef tapped his pack.

"Thanks again for bringing it," he said.

"Wasn't sure how things would turn out," Renni said. "But I thought it might be my only chance to get it to you, even if we couldn't get you out of the underworld."

Then the goodbyes had all been said and Intef, Sabu and I walked away. I sniffled, trying not to let my tears fall.

"Cry if you need to," Intef said. "I know it will hurt you to be separated from Istnofret in particular."

I nodded. If I tried to speak right now, I would burst into tears and I didn't want to cry in front of Sabu. Our arrival at the dock was a welcome distraction. Three ships prepared to leave and their crews hurried as they loaded the last supplies. Intef pointed out the one we were to travel on and we waited nearby until told to board.

The captain was a Greek man and seemed somewhat suspicious of me. However, Intef had made it clear that a woman would be travelling with him and although the captain was clearly unhappy about it, he was already resigned to my presence. He pointed out where we were to wait while the ship disembarked and we set our packs down in a tidy pile.

Intef sat beside me, while Sabu leaned over the bulkhead and stared out at the water. It seemed Intef wouldn't be working with the crew this time. We had no shortage of gems to pay our way, despite the ones left in the tunnels.

The journey took a day longer than it should have as the wind died midway and we had to wait for most of a day until the sails caught the breeze again. The captain spent the hours staring alternately at the sky and at me. I supposed he blamed the presence of a woman onboard for the wind dropping.

I pretended I wasn't bothered, but I spent almost as much time watching the sky as the captain did. Even now, I wasn't sure I remembered everything about the day I drowned, but I did remember the storm. There was no sign of bad weather, though, just a complete absence of wind.

The captain prowled across the deck until we caught the wind again. After nine days, we finally heard that the Egyptian coastline had been sighted.

"Almost home, Shadow," I murmured. It stretched across the deck, long in the afternoon sun. "It will be good to be back on Egyptian soil again, will it not?"

I knew it couldn't respond, but we had forged a new level of trust during our time in the tunnels, and I intended to keep my promise this time. I found a strange comfort in talking to it, this being that could neither respond nor even move unless I did, and yet it thought and felt and loved. It gave me a deep sense of peace to know my shadow heard me.

As we drew closer to the Egyptian coast, I made out the ships which milled around the harbour.

"There are an awful lot of ships," I said to Intef as we stood together at the bow.

He shaded his eyes with his hand to get a better view.

"They are not Egyptian ships." His voice was grim. "The Hittites have arrived."

THIRTY-FIVE

My *father is incensed.* That was what the Hittite princess Muwatti said in her last letter. *He has sworn he will obliterate Egypt.*

I had sent a messenger to Suppiluliumas with an apology for the death of his son, Zannanza, who had been on his way to marry me when Ay had him killed. The messenger took with him what I now realised was an insultingly paltry compensation: one hundred rolls of linen, one hundred *shabti*, one hundred woven baskets, one hundred beads. I should have sent one thousand of each. Maybe even ten thousand. I had offended Suppiluliumas and he came to avenge his son's death. There were dozens of Hittite war ships waiting to dock, maybe as many as a hundred.

"This is my fault," I whispered.

"I wonder if Horemheb knows?" Intef said. "If they have only just arrived, word may not have even reached Memphis yet."

"What do we do?"

While we sailed, I had told him that resolving the threat of war was the last thing I intended to do. Had promised we would make a new life together once this was done.

"I suppose Suppiluliumas is here somewhere," he said. "If he has taken this as personally as you think, he would come himself."

"He is supposed to be a reasonable man," I said. "Perhaps if I could explain, he might understand it was all a terrible misunderstanding."

Sabu came to stand with us and look out at the ships.

"Hittites?" he asked.

"I think so," Intef said. "The hulls are not braced with ropes like our ships. Also look at the sternposts. See how they rise and curve over?"

"So you are going to try to speak with their king?" Sabu asked me.

He, too, knew I needed to make peace with Suppiluliumas. He hadn't exactly said he would help, but he also hadn't said he wouldn't. I supposed he was waiting to see what the situation was when we arrived before he decided.

"He might seize the opportunity to make an example of you in retribution for his son's death," Intef said before I could answer.

"I have to risk it," I said.

"You might not get close to him," he said. "Not without being captured."

"I will do what I must. I have to set this right. This is the last thing, Intef. Once this is done, we can live our own lives."

"I hope so," he said. "I don't want to live like this anymore, Samun. I am too old for it."

I was thirty years old by now and Intef must be thirty-two. We weren't old, but we were far from young either. In another ten years, we would indeed be old. It seemed like a lifetime ago that I sat on the wooden bench in my pleasure garden in Akhetaten and watched the ducks splash in the lake while I thought about how I was the only imperfect thing there. That must have been thirteen years ago.

"I already promised you," I said. "This is the last thing."

"Well, then. What is your plan?"

"I need to speak with Suppiluliumas in person."

"How do you intend to do that without being captured?" he asked.

"Perhaps being captured is exactly what I need."

"They might not let a prisoner speak with the king," Sabu said.

Intef nodded. "It fact, I would think it is unlikely. They might permit you to speak with one of his captains, but nobody higher."

"If Arnuwanda is here, he might arrange for me to speak with

Suppiluliumas," I said. "After all, when he captured me in Armenia, he was taking me to see the king."

"Or he said he was, perhaps to ensure your compliance," Intef said. "It is easier to transport a willing prisoner."

"But once Suppiluliumas knows his men have me, he will want to speak with me. I wrote to him. He knows who I am. He knows my brother and my father. He would want to see me even if only to tell me he blames me for Zannanza's death."

"Be careful, Samun. Your plan assumes he sees you as having some authority. But you are no longer queen. He may treat you no better than a commoner."

"But even if I am not queen, I am still a princess. My father was Pharaoh, as was my brother. Suppiluliumas will speak with me."

"If they even tell him who you are," he said. "They might choose not to. They might not believe you."

"Arnuwanda will recognise me."

"Arnuwanda might not be here. He may no longer be alive or he may not still be in favour. Your plan relies on too many assumptions."

"So give me a better plan then," I said. "One without assumptions."

He sighed. "I cannot. You must find a way to speak with Suppiluliumas, and I can think of no way to achieve that without relying on your name."

I looked to Sabu in case he had any ideas, but he only shrugged. We were now close enough to see the men on board the warships. Some were obviously crew, preparing to leave the ship. Others were soldiers, preparing for battle.

Almost a full day passed before we could disembark, such was the line of ships ahead of us. Before we left, we put on clean clothes, although there was no fresh water left in which to bathe. With our hair brushed and kohl around our eyes, we looked more or less Egyptian again. At last, we stood on land.

"I never thought to set foot in Egypt again," Intef said. "What season is this? *Shemu*?"

"It was mid *peret* when we left," I said. "We have only been gone a few weeks." Too early for the harvest time to have arrived, but close to it.

"I missed the heat," Sabu said.

"I missed the endless skies," Intef added. "Sunlight bouncing off stone and sand." He laughed. "I remember how much I hated the sand when I was a boy and my father moved us to Akhetaten. It seemed to find its way everywhere and it made me itch. I suppose I got used to it eventually."

The dock was busy with men carrying crates of weapons or supplies. Others barked orders. Rhakotis was normally filled with people of different nationalities, as is usual for harbour towns, but today I saw only Hittites.

"What do we do?" I asked. "How do I get to Suppiluliumas?"

Intef studied the men surrounding us.

"We need whoever is the most senior here," he said. "He will be able to pass word on. There, that man."

Intef nodded towards a man who stood in the shade of a dom palm tree. He looked like any other Hittite, with a muscular body and a thick black beard. He wore something like a *shendyt* with a tunic and a leather belt bristling with daggers around his waist. Beside him, a spear rested against the trunk of the dom palm. He watched the men with careful eyes that seemed to miss nothing.

"How do you know he is the captain?" I asked. "He is not giving orders. He hasn't even spoken to anyone."

"He shouldn't need to give orders if his men are well trained. But look at how he watches them. He knows what he expects and he is watching for any deviation."

"So, do I go up to him and introduce myself?"

Now the moment had come, I doubted my plan. What if he didn't speak Akkadian, which was the only language I knew other than Egyptian? What if he had me arrested and locked away? Or he didn't believe me and just ignored me?

"I suppose so," Intef said. "It is all on you, though. There is little I can do to help since I don't speak any Akkadian myself."

"Me either," Sabu said.

"I think you should both wait here," I said. "If it goes badly, he might imprison you, too, if he sees you with me."

"It is too late," Intef said. "He has already seen us."

Indeed, I glanced up as the man's gaze drifted over us. He seemed to pay us no particular attention, though.

"I am not sure he noticed us," I said. "He is looking at everything."

"Oh, he has noticed," Intef said. "He would not be much of a captain if not. He knows we are talking about him and he likely waits for you to approach, so you may as well go do it."

"Wish me luck then," I said.

"May Isis protect you."

He squeezed my hand, then gave me a little push in the captain's direction.

THIRTY-SIX

The captain didn't seem to notice as I made my way between his soldiers. However, as I reached him, I realised he watched me out of the corner of his eye. Intef was right. The man paid attention to everything. When I stopped in front of him, he raised one hand to wave me away.

"We have our own women with us," he said in Akkadian. "We have no need for local women."

By the goddess. He thought I was here to offer myself to his men. Flustered, it took me a few moments too long to think of a reply. He looked at me again and raised his eyebrows.

"Are you deaf? Or simple."

"I wish to speak with your king," I said.

He made a noise of amusement.

"I am sure you do, but I am afraid you will have to get in line. There are likely many who wish to speak with him."

"Can you get a message to him for me?"

"Why would I do that?"

"Because he will want to see me once he knows I am here."

I expected he would ask my name, but his mouth twitched and he looked away again, maintaining his careful watch over his men.

"Unless you are Pharaoh, I doubt my king has any wish to speak with you," he said.

"Is the princess Muwatti here?"

He shot me a sharp look.

"What do you know of the princess?" he asked.

"I have corresponded with her. She is favourably inclined towards me."

She had written to warn me of her father's anger at any rate.

"The princess is safely at home, as all respectable women should be," he said.

I ignored the barb.

"Then let me speak with the king. How do I get a message to him?"

"You do not."

Perhaps that had been a poor choice of words.

"How do you get a message to him?" I asked.

"I do not."

"Then how does anyone speak to the king?"

I felt his irritation. He wanted me to leave so he could focus on his men. But I was determined not to walk away until I had a way of contacting Suppiluliumas.

"You would have to get a message to Arnuwanda," he said at last. "He controls what messages are presented to the king."

"I know Arnuwanda. Where is he?"

He gave me a look, amused at last.

"With the king, of course," he said.

"And where is that?"

"I have no idea. I know only what I need to and I do not need to know the king's location."

"Then where is your captain? Is he of sufficient rank to know where the king is? Or is he also too junior?"

He bristled, and one hand went to a dagger at his waist. He took a deep breath and calmed himself.

"What do you want, woman? I have things to do, and I do not have time to converse with you."

"I have already told you what I want. To speak with the king."

"And I have told you that is not possible."

"No, you told me you don't think your king will want to speak with me. An assumption, of course, about something which you have no knowledge of."

His nostrils flared and his fingers tightened around the dagger handle.

"Unless you want to end this day as a prisoner of war, I suggest you remove yourself from my presence," he said.

"Would being a prisoner get me in front of the king?"

He barked a command in his own language and two soldiers came to take me by the arms.

"I hope you know what you are doing." The captain glared at me.

"I hope you have the sense to know that when someone demands a message be passed to your king, you should do so."

He snapped out another command, and the soldiers tugged on my arms to lead me away. I glanced over my shoulder, but Intef and Sabu had disappeared. If they had not been captured, they might find a way to get to Suppiluliumas if I was unsuccessful.

The soldiers confined me to a cottage whose owners must have either been kicked out or fled at the army's arrival. It comprised only a single chamber with a soldier to guard the open door. But I had some privacy, which was unexpected for a prisoner, and the previous inhabitants had left everything when they fled, so I had a lamp and oil and a bed mat. There was not much to eat, but I found the end of a loaf of bread and some beer. It would be enough for tonight, at least.

I felt wide awake and was sure I wouldn't sleep for a moment. But I must have drifted off, for I soon found myself in a dream about Suppiluliumas. I recognised him from when I had dreamed about him before, although this dream was different.

I saw Suppiluliumas lying in a bed. His face was pale, gaunt and sweaty. He raised one arm, although it seemed to take an enormous effort, and gestured for someone to come closer. Then the dream changed and Suppiluliumas was well and whole. He smiled as a woman approached and handed him a swaddled babe.

In the first dream, Suppiluliumas was clearly unwell, but I couldn't tell whether he suffered from a battle wound or an illness. Perhaps this dream showed that if he stayed to fight in Egypt, he would die. In the other fate ahead of him, someone handed him a babe. His own child, perhaps? Or a grandchild? I saw little of his surroundings in the second dream, but surely this must occur after he returned to Hattusa.

If only I could see what happened before those two fates. Osiris said I could learn to control them, but how? I needed to know whether either of these fates would be a result of war. My dreams had only ever shown what would occur because of a decision I myself made. But how could I know which fate would be better without knowing whether Suppiluliumas first laid waste to Egypt, as his daughter warned me he intended?

THIRTY-SEVEN

I didn't sleep again after my dream about Suppiluliumas. I tried to tell myself to go back to sleep and to dream of what happened prior to the two fates I saw, but I was wide awake.

Remembering the old woman who showed me images in a bowl of water, I searched the cottage for a suitable vessel. The inhabitants didn't have a bronze bowl like hers, but I found a small wooden bowl and half a bucket of water. I sat staring into the water for a long time but never saw even the slightest flicker of an image.

By the time a soldier came to get me, I had been awake for hours. He didn't speak, just gestured for me to go with him. Perhaps he knew we didn't speak any language in common. He took a firm hold of my arm and led me to a pair of oxen hitched to a cart. He gestured for me to climb in and tied a rope around my wrist. Then he fastened the other end to the rail at the front of the cart. He obviously didn't understand I was a willing prisoner.

The soldier climbed up onto the front seat and a wiry old Egyptian man got in beside him. So, perhaps the cart was hired rather than commandeered. Or perhaps the man was a traitor.

We drove through the streets of Rhakotis. I knew Suppiluliumas must have bought many soldiers with him — I saw how many ships he had — but even so, I was shocked at just how many Hittites were here. They seemed to be everywhere. The usual inhabitants of Rhakotis were nowhere to be seen. Perhaps they stayed within their homes or perhaps they had fled. As we drove past one particular house, I spotted a young girl standing at the front door. She was only three or four years old and she stood with her thumb in her mouth as she watched the soldiers. An arm emerged from the house and dragged her inside. The door closed behind her.

We drove right through the town without stopping. Perhaps we were going to the Great River. Suppiluliumas might have already left for Memphis. The cart came to a halt and while I waited for the soldier to come and release me, I took a careful look at the knot securing my wrist. Could I undo it myself if they had forgotten about me? But the knot was expertly tied, and it only took one look to know I would not undo it without both hands, and perhaps not even then. They hadn't taken my pouch from me, though, and hopefully my dagger was where it should be. I could cut the rope if I needed to.

The soldier untied the rope where it was fastened to the cart. He left the other end around my wrist and tugged to indicate I should follow him. I climbed down, my back and legs stiff after the long ride.

Since he had me secured with the rope, the soldier didn't bother to take my arm this time. He escorted me through the crowd of Hittites as if I was a cow being led to market. Although my cheeks burned with humiliation, nobody seemed to take any notice. The men here were soldiers preparing to fight. They stood in orderly rows, clutching daggers and vicious-looking swords shaped like crescent moons. A few were praying and others talked quietly between themselves, but most were silent as they waited for orders.

The soldier led me right through the men and up to the edge of what appeared to be a battlefield. On the far side of the field stood the Egyptian army. Our men clutched spears and shields and were far less orderly than the Hittite army. They didn't stand in rows which were as neat and most didn't seem to pay any attention to the men waiting on the other side of the field. I wasn't tall enough to see how many Egyptians were here. Surely there had been no time to raise an army large enough to answer the Hittites' arrival adequately.

I was so intent on examining our army that I didn't realise the soldier had stopped until I crashed into him. He turned to glare at me. It was then I saw Arnuwanda. The soldier gave him a lengthy explanation, although he didn't speak in Akkadian, so I had no idea what he said. Arnuwanda listened and seemed to indicate the man could leave. The soldier handed him the rope and departed without even a backward glance at me. The fate of a prisoner was clearly of no concern to him.

Arnuwanda looked me up and down. Perhaps he tried to reconcile this version of me with what he had seen before. He looked more haggard than I remembered. I had thought he was nothing more than an envoy the first time we met, but it seemed he controlled access to the king. Perhaps he was more senior than I understood, or perhaps he had been promoted. Either way, I should treat him with respect. He was the one person here who could give me what I wanted if the captain had spoken the truth. I bowed my head.

"Good day to you," I said in Akkadian. "I am here to speak with Suppiluliumas."

Arnuwanda shook his head.

"A bold statement for one who is a prisoner standing on the edge of a battlefield."

"There has been a terrible misunderstanding. You, of all people, know what my intent was. You know I was serious about marrying a prince of the Hittites and making him pharaoh."

"I know what you said and I know what happened afterwards. Those two things do not seem to tally."

"I was not responsible for Zannanza's death. I have told you this before."

"Yes, you claim to have no involvement. And yet when my king did as you asked, when he sent one of our dearly beloved sons to you, he was murdered. You asked for a son of the Hittites, you received one, and you killed him."

"I did not kill him. I had no knowledge that such a thing would happen. He was murdered, yes, but not on my order. If he had reached me, I would have married him. He would have been pharaoh."

"And yet someone took care to ensure he did not reach you. Mmm?"

"I took the throne from the man responsible and exiled him from Memphis. He will never again hold any position of authority in Egypt. He will never again be able to do such a terrible thing."

"My king does not care about what may or may not happen in the future," Arnuwanda said. "He cares only that his son was murdered and he has sworn vengeance on Egypt."

"May I speak with him? Please? If I could just explain what happened—"

"He already knows what happened, and you have given me no reason why I should present your case to him. The man you murdered was not only my king's son. He was also my brother."

So Arnuwanda was Suppiluliumas's son. No wonder he had risen to such a high status. Before I could acknowledge this, Arnuwanda continued.

"My king is too busy for conversation this morning. As you can see, he prepares to send our army into battle."

"There does not need to be a battle. We can still resolve this amicably. I sent him compensation, but I now realise it wasn't enough. If Suppiluliumas would tell me what he wants, I will see that he gets whatever it is. We will compensate him for the loss of his son to whatever value he requires."

Arnuwanda looked me up and down.

"Are you in a position to give such assurances? My understanding is that you are no longer queen."

"I am not, but I know both Pharaoh and his queen well. She is my mother's sister and they will listen to me. Ask Suppiluliumas what he wants and I will tell Pharaoh to give it to him."

Arnuwanda snapped a command in his own language and handed my rope to a man behind him. A servant perhaps. He didn't look like a soldier. He watched me with serious eyes as Arnuwanda walked away.

When Arnuwanda finally returned, he looked far too amused to bring any serious reply.

"My king sends his thanks for your offer and he will be pleased to accept," he said without preamble.

My hopes lifted.

"What does he want? Tell me and I will make it happen."

"My king has no more desire than you to engage in battle today. These are his demands. If they are met by sundown, he will send his army back to the ships and we will depart peacefully. He wants ten thousand slaughtered cattle. Their carcasses are to be piled in the field here between the armies and burned until nothing remains."

How would I ever gather up ten thousand cattle before sunset? It would take an army to do such a thing. Perhaps somewhere in the Egyptian army that waited here might be a captain that Intef or Sabu knew. We might be able to convince them to have the army help us.

But Arnuwanda wasn't finished.

"He wants ten thousand *deben* of good grain," he said. "Nothing that is mouldy or infested with vermin. It, too, is to be placed in the field and burned. Finally, he wants ten thousand Egyptian children under the age of ten. They, too, will be placed in the field and burned. As my king is merciful, he has agreed their throats may be cut before their bodies are burned."

THIRTY-EIGHT

For a few moments, I could do nothing other than stare at Arnuwanda.

"You cannot be serious," I said.

"My king is very serious. Now tell me, will your Pharaoh comply or are we engaging in battle today?"

My mouth opened and closed. The cattle and grain were one matter. With enough time, we could gather what he wanted, even if the request was vindictive. He didn't want resources to take back to his own country. He wanted to bankrupt us and leave our people to starve. On some level, I could understand. He had, after all, come to destroy us.

It was the children that staggered me. This was beyond vindictive. Beyond any level of revenge a person might think was a reasonable entitlement for the loss of a son.

"Surely he doesn't think we should murder ten thousand children to atone for the death of one son," I said. "Is this supposed to be a joke?"

Arnuwanda gave me a stony stare.

"I should have thought by now, Ankhesenamun, formerly Queen of Egypt, you would know I do not joke. I relayed your request to my king and these are his demands. If you wish to avoid war today, you will comply. Otherwise my king says it will please him to decimate your army. Then he will take the ten thousand oxen and the ten thousand *deben* of grain and the ten thousand children, anyway. Your only decision is whether we must slaughter your army first."

Perhaps he was serious. Perhaps I offended him more than I realised with my offer of one hundred each of linens, *shabti*, woven baskets and beads.

"But ten thousand children?" I asked. "It is inconceivable. Pharaoh will not agree to such a thing."

"Are you certain you can speak for your Pharaoh? If that is his response, I will convey it to my king. If we are to battle today, better that we begin while the day is young."

"Let me talk to Suppiluliumas myself. Please."

"He has made his decision. My king does not change his mind."

"Would he accept one life?"

I couldn't promise other lives, especially those of children, but I could give my own if it would be the difference between war or not. I was raised to expect to serve my pharaoh with my life and my body. This was no more than I owed.

Arnuwanda looked at me for so long that I thought he would refuse.

"A counter offer," he said at last. "A paltry one, but perhaps my king will wish to consider it. I will relay it to him."

"No, please, let me tell him myself. If I am to offer my life for that of his son, let me at least make the request in person."

Arnuwanda shrugged. "All I can do is ask him. It is his decision whether he will speak with you."

"Thank you."

I supposed it was the best I could hope for.

Arnuwanda led me to a pavilion guarded by a full squad. He spoke to a guard and handed him my rope. Then he disappeared inside.

A roar of laughter reached my ears. Arnuwanda held aside the curtain and gestured for me to enter. He took my rope back from the guard and handed it to me, then went to wait outside. I had thought he would be there with me when I faced his father.

The pavilion was a basic structure, just a number of hides stitched together and fastened to poles. Lamps hung from the poles provided both light and an unwelcome amount of heat. Thick rugs covered the bare dirt. Several chairs and a table were positioned near to each other and there sat a man I had seen only in my dreams.

Suppululiumas looked much like any other Hittite, although he carried himself with a noble bearing that was unmistakable. Even lounging in a chair with a mug in his hand, he gave off an aura of competence and decisiveness. Anyone who saw him would recognise he was important, even if they didn't know he was a king.

I prostrated myself on the rug. Regardless of my former position, I was no more than a suppliant. I wasn't even an official representative of the government, despite what I told Arnuwanda.

"Rise." His tone was curt, the merriness I heard when he laughed at Arnuwanda absent.

I got to my feet and waited. In Egypt, a servant shouldn't speak before their betters. I didn't know whether the Hittites had a similar custom, but he would not view politeness unfavourably.

"So it is not enough for you to murder my son, then insult me with the letter carried by your messenger," Suppululiumas said. "You come to insult me to my face also?"

"I seek only to explain, your majesty. If you will permit me."

"You intend to explain why you murdered my son, who I sent to you at your guarantee of his safety? I think we are beyond the point of any explanation."

"I truly intended to marry him. As Isis is my witness, everything I wrote to you was the truth."

He drained his mug and a servant dashed in to refill it. I was acutely aware he hadn't offered me any refreshments. He didn't view me as a visitor worthy of respect.

"Go on, then," he said. "Since I have travelled all this way and you are here in front of me, tell me what it is you think I do not know about my son's murder. Then my army will decimate your country. You will be a laughingstock among nations. Never again will any king listen to your lies. All will know of Egypt's treachery by the time I am finished."

I took a deep breath. Despite his insults, he had at least said I could explain.

"Your majesty, after I wrote to ask that you send me one of your sons, the throne was taken from me by force. The new pharaoh forged my signature on a marriage certificate and claimed the throne as my husband. He then wanted an excuse to get rid of me, and your son's arrival at our border was exactly what he needed. He claimed your son led an army coming to invade us and ordered them all to be slaughtered."

"My son travelled with an escort of fifty soldiers." Suppiluliumas's face was red. "Who would try to invade any country with so few men, let alone Egypt, which is renowned for the size of its armies?"

"It was a lie and anyone who knew just how few men travelled with Zannanza would see it. But our people are not accustomed to hearing lies from their pharaoh. If Pharaoh says something, they believe it."

"So, if you were the only person who knew the truth, what did you do about it?"

"They confined me to my chambers for some months afterwards and permitted me to have no contact with anyone other than my serving women and my own guards."

"So you did nothing."

"What would you have me do from within the walls of my chambers? I was not allowed out. Not to go for a walk. Not to sit in the sun. Nothing."

"Surely you could have gotten a message out via your guards? Could they not have spread the word about what your pharaoh had done?"

"Who would believe them? And who would be able to do anything about it? Pharaoh's word is law. People loyal to him would have reported my men for spreading lies about Pharaoh. It would do nothing but endanger my guards. I judged it best to wait until Pharaoh released me. I thought I would be able to do something then."

"So you put your own interests ahead of spreading the truth."

He laughed, although scornfully, likely too angry to be amused.

"The truth," I said, somewhat bitterly, "is whatever Pharaoh says it is. Perhaps things are different in Hattusa. Perhaps your people may question the words of their king. If that is so, then you may not understand, but if Pharaoh says the wind blows upwards from the ground and that the sand is blue, it is truth. Anyone who says otherwise is considered a heretic and a traitor."

Suppiluliumas studied me for some time. I drew back my shoulders and held my head high, determined not to show him how afraid I was. At least he couldn't see how my legs trembled.

"As for the compensation I sent you, I realise now that it was vastly insufficient," I said. "I was not myself at that time and although I thought it was adequate compensation, I see now I was wrong."

I made myself stop talking. I had said everything I needed to. Suppiluliumas studied me for a long time.

"I find I am inclined to believe your words," he said, at last.

My relief was short-lived.

"So I will say this: I accept your counter offer of one life for that of my son. Bring me the man who ordered my son's death. He will pay with his life and I will call the exchange fair enough. If you do this, my army will retreat."

"He is gone," I said. "Exiled. When I was finally able to take the throne back from him, I sent him away from Memphis. I do not know where he went."

"Then you had better find him. I will give you one day. Bring him to me by this time tomorrow and we will depart peacefully. Otherwise, we will destroy your army. We will burn your crops and enslave your people. Egypt will never again be an independent nation, but will forever be ruled by the Hittites. And my descendants will know that I, Suppiluliumas, crushed Egypt as if it were an ant."

THIRTY-NINE

Suppiluliumas gestured, and someone grabbed my arms from behind. They hauled me backwards out of the pavilion, just like in my dream. Arnuwanda led me back to the edge of the army, then he untied my rope and disappeared into the crowd without a word.

Intef and Sabu must have been hiding somewhere nearby and they appeared as soon as Arnuwanda left. Intef knew from the look on my face that it wasn't good news.

"What happened?" he asked. "Were you harmed?"

"He didn't hurt me. He is here to get his revenge for Zannanza's death."

"As we thought," he said.

"He has made me an offer, a way to avoid war. If I give him Ay, he will call off his army and retreat."

"Do you know where Ay is?" he asked.

"Not a clue. I told him to leave Memphis and never return. I didn't give any instructions about where he was to go, just that it should be away."

"So he may not even be in Egypt?"

"I have one day to find him."

"Might the timeframe be negotiable?" Sabu asked.

"No," I said. "Suppiluliumas thinks he is being generous. I didn't even have a chance to ask any questions. He made his offer and guards led me away immediately. I fear if I asked for more time, he might shorten it."

"So we have one day," Intef said.

"Not enough time to get a message to Memphis, let alone receive a reply," Sabu said.

"From what Samun has said, I think it is unlikely Horemheb would know where Ay went anyway," Intef said. "He probably left with no plan of where he was going."

"What about his advisors?" I asked. "Maya and Wennefer. Perhaps he has been in contact with them?"

"Do we know where they might be?" Intef asked.

"I would guess they stayed in the vicinity of Memphis," Sabu said. "They both have family and friends there. So we cannot get to them in time either. Who else might he contact?"

"You know his personal squad better than I do," Intef said. "Would he reach out to any of them?"

Sabu shook his head. "They were not fond of him, not even our captain, Nehi."

"There is one person I can think of who seemed to value Ay," I said. "An administrator, quite senior, I think. A fat man. Intef, I am sure you will know who I mean. He was there the day I went to confront Ay after he decided to move the capital to Memphis."

"Bak." Intef's voice was flat. "A spectacularly untalented man, but rather good at flattery, which of course, Ay liked."

"Do you know where he is?" I asked Sabu, but he shook his head.

"He is no longer in Memphis as far as I know," he said. "But anyway, he was just an administrator. Ay would not maintain contact with someone he considered inferior."

"You are right." I sighed. "But Bak is the only person I can think of who might still want to know him."

"Let's find some accommodation," Intef said. "We need somewhere to rest and to talk in private."

It didn't take long to find a house we could hire for a few days. After our experience in the tunnels, it was still a relief to have walls around me. As I spread out a blanket to sit on, a thought struck me.

"Oh, I am an idiot," I said. "I forgot about his wife."

Intef slapped himself on the forehead.

"By the gods, I am rusty after being away for so long. What do we know about her?"

"Her name is Tey."

I could hardly forget her name — it was the same as Intef's sister, who gave up her life in Akhetaten to shepherd my sisters to safety. If Isis blessed Intef and me with another daughter some day, I should call her Tey.

"Her family was from somewhere south of Memphis," Intef said. "I cannot recall where, but let me think for a bit. It will come to me."

"Akhmin," Sabu said. "I was assigned to her squad at one point when there were too many men out sick. Remember that sweating illness where folk were ill for a week or more? We feared it was a return of the Asiatic Plague. Anyway, I heard the queen talking about receiving a letter from her mother and sending a messenger to Akhmin with a reply."

"How far away is that?" I asked.

"Too far," Intef said. "Past Akhetaten, almost as far as Thebes."

"I don't think the queen's family is still there," Sabu said. "Didn't they move to Buto a couple of years ago? That is not far from here. If her family is there, she might be also, and so might Ay. Do we have time to go there?"

"It is at least a full day's walk from here, I think," Intef said. "We might make it in half a day with a cart and a couple of oxen."

"Let's go now." I started to get up, feeling quite refreshed at this news.

"Stay here and rest," Intef said. "I will find transport. No point us all going."

He slipped away, leaving just Sabu and I.

"He is right that we should rest while we can," Sabu said. "It will likely be a long day."

He lay on a blanket and seemed to fall asleep quickly. I lay down, too, and stared up at the ceiling. If only I had the forethought to tell Ay to go somewhere specific, this would be much easier. But how could I have known I would need to find him? I never expected to see him again, much less seek him out.

Intef returned an hour or so later.

"Couldn't find anyone willing to loan or sell a cart," he said. "But I bought some donkeys."

"It is better than walking." Sabu was already on his feet.

"Let's take enough supplies to last us until tomorrow, and the gems, of course," Intef said. "Leave everything else here. The lighter we travel, the better it will be for the donkeys."

He had purchased six beasts so we could rest each in turn. We set off and for some time I was occupied with holding on and trying not to fall off. I hadn't ridden a donkey since the night the medjay rescued me on the way to the slave mines. Eventually, I settled into the ride and could turn my thoughts to finding Ay.

"What will we do if Tey's family isn't still in Bhuto?" I asked. "I assume we hope they will tell us where Tey is and that when we find her, we will find Ay. But what if they cannot or will not tell us? We don't have time to go anywhere else if they are not there."

"We will worry about that when we get there," Intef said. "I would find it difficult to believe her family doesn't know where she is. There are ways of making a person talk even if they don't want to."

"You intend to torture them?" It was only after I spoke that I realised how judgemental I sounded, although it wasn't intentional. "I mean, do you think that might be necessary?"

"I think we need to do whatever we must to find Ay," Intef said. "If we can avoid war with the Hittites by turning him over to them, then I will do anything I must to make that happen."

"As will I," Sabu said. "He is not worth protecting at the expense of the rest of the country."

"So what do we do once we find him?" I asked. "He will not come with us willingly."

"We need to find him first, and that may not be easy," Intef said. "There might well be those who will warn him if they learn we are looking for him. But once we find him, I expect we will have to force him to come with us. We can tie him onto a donkey and take him back to Rhakotis. It is a pity I couldn't get more than six donkeys. We won't be able to rest the poor beasts enough if they need to carry four of us."

It was early afternoon before we reached Bhuto. We found a busy marketplace with a well and some shady trees nearby. We tied the donkeys' halters onto branches so they couldn't wander away and drew up some water from the well for them.

"I will go see what I can find out," Intef said as the donkeys drank. "Perhaps find a place where people gather to gossip. I might hear something useful."

"Surely it is unlikely anyone will be talking about Tey's family just as you pass by to overhear it," I said.

"Trust me, Samun. I am well accustomed to getting information out of people without them realising the importance of what they tell me."

After he left, Sabu sat where he could lean against a tree. He groaned.

"Are you well, Sabu?" I asked.

"Well enough," he said. "I have never ridden a beast before and it was not a comfortable experience. I am not sorry to have a chance to sit for a while."

He closed his eyes and didn't seem inclined to converse further. I sat against another tree.

"Well, Shadow," I said, softly so as not to disturb Sabu. "I wonder how you found the donkey ride? I am not sure I will ever get used to such a thing."

Intef was gone for a long time, and I dozed while I waited. When he returned, he looked rather dejected.

"Nothing," he said glumly, as he dropped down to sit beside me. "I thought that since Tey was the daughter of a local family, there might be all sorts of gossip, particularly if she had recently returned to her family. But if anyone knows, they are not speaking. I asked a few questions, but folk clammed up as soon as they realised who I wanted to know about. There seems to be a lot of loyalty to the family and nobody is willing to talk about them."

"Intef," Sabu said.

"I see him," Intef replied. "I am giving him time to decide what he will do. If he slips away, I will follow and see if I can find out what he wants."

"Who?" I looked around, but saw nobody nearby.

"Don't look," Intef said. "Someone followed me back from the market. He might intend to report to the family that I've been asking questions."

I finally spotted the fellow. He was a lanky young man, perhaps in his early twenties. He loitered some distance from us, apparently trying to pretend he hadn't seen us and merely waited for someone. Eventually, he started towards us.

Even though Intef had his back to the fellow, I could tell he knew of his approach. He waited until the fellow was no more than the length of a couple of men from us before he got to his feet.

FORTY

"Following me?" Intef asked the man.

His tone was pleasant enough and only someone who knew him well might recognise the warning in it. The fellow wrung his hands and glanced back over his shoulder.

"Nobody followed you," Intef said. "However, I was aware you were following me long before I left the market."

"You gave no sign you saw me." The man was sweating profusely and he wiped his forehead with his sleeve.

"What do you want?" Intef asked.

Sabu got to his feet and wandered off. Perhaps he checked if anyone else was approaching or perhaps he was trying to get around behind the fellow in case he turned out to be a threat. Either way, I was sure his wandering was not as aimless as it seemed.

"I heard you were asking questions," the man said.

"Is that a crime here in Bhuto?" Intef asked.

"No, no, of course not. It is just that, well, certain people don't like anyone asking questions about them. They pay people to listen out for such things."

"And might you be one of those people paid to listen?"

"No, no. I am… no friend to them."

"What did they do to you?"

"I wanted to marry one of the daughters of the family." His voice was bitter. "Her father refused me because my status is not high enough. I am only a farmer and he wants better than that for his daughter. He will not allow her to be a farmer's wife."

"So you are looking to share information about the family?"

Intef's voice was carefully neutral. Whatever he might think of the fellow's motives, he wasn't letting on.

"No, of course not. I merely thought... well, you look like you want something pretty bad and I thought you might be able to pay for it. You know? If I was wealthier, her father might be more receptive."

"I might pay for information," Intef said. "But it would have to be good information. Very good."

"Are you looking for the family, or is it the queen you want? Because I know where she is."

I inhaled sharply, then realised I might have just told him how valuable his information was. I tried to cover my mistake by coughing.

Intef shrugged.

"I would need more than that," he said.

"You will not hurt anyone, will you?" the fellow asked. "I wouldn't want to be party to something like that, since I'm trying to marry into the family and all."

"I don't intend to hurt anyone."

"Right. Well, then. I can take you to where she lives."

"Is that the best you can do?" Intef asked.

The fellow swallowed hard.

"What more would you want?" he asked. "You aren't, um, you aren't looking for Pharaoh, are you? That is, the man who used to be Pharaoh? There is a man living with the queen. I don't know who he is. I never saw Pharaoh myself, you understand. But they seem quite familiar with each other and I wondered whether he might have been Pharaoh."

Intef reached into a pack. He pulled out a gem, tossed it into the air and caught it, then held it up for the fellow to inspect.

"You take us to this man," he said. "If it is indeed Pharaoh, this is yours."

The fellow's eyes went round.

"Is it…" He swallowed. "It is a real sapphire, yes?"

"Oh, it is real," Intef said. "And it is yours if the man you speak of is the one we seek."

"How do I know you will be honest with me?" the fellow asked. "I could take you to him and you might say, oh no, it is the wrong man and not give me anything."

Intef shrugged and dropped the gem back into his pack.

"I suppose you need to decide for yourself whether to trust us. It will not be hard to find someone else willing to help. I care little who the gem goes to so long as I get the information I seek."

The fellow hesitated, his gaze still fixed on Intef's pack.

"You swear to the gods you are being straight with me?" he asked.

"You have my word," Intef said.

"All right then. I will come back tonight. After dark."

"No, you can show me now."

Likely he thought the fellow would change his mind once he left us.

"Wait here," Intef said to me and Sabu. "I will be back as soon as I can."

They left and Sabu looked after them with a worried expression.

"Maybe I should follow them," he suggested. "He might be trying to get Intef on his own so he can steal the gem."

I scoffed.

"He can try, but it would take more than one man to take Intef down, even with only one arm."

Still, Intef and the fellow were almost out of sight.

"Let's go," I said. "We will stay well back from them. Intef will notice, but as long as we don't get in the way, he won't mind too much."

"What about the donkeys?" Sabu asked.

I had forgotten the donkeys. We would need them to get Ay back to Rhakotis if we found him.

"You stay here," I said. "I will follow Intef."

"And what will you do if he is in trouble? A woman, alone?"

I bristled.

"Intef has taught me to defend myself and I have done it on more than one occasion."

Sabu gave me a doubtful look and shook his head.

"I don't think Intef would appreciate me allowing you to put yourself in danger like that. Either I go after them or we both stay here."

"No," I said. "You stay."

I darted away before he could reply. I didn't think he would risk leaving the donkeys to come after me.

In the time Sabu and I spent arguing, Intef and the fellow had disappeared. I hurried in the direction they went and soon caught sight of them. I followed at a distance, trying to keep close to the walls of the buildings we passed. If the fellow noticed, he gave no sign of it. Intef cast a quick glance back at one point. He must have seen me, although he didn't acknowledge it. I could hardly expect him to, and what could he say to me from this distance, anyway? It wasn't the first time I regretted not knowing the language of hand signals he and Renni used when they needed to communicate silently.

As we made our way through the town, the houses became bigger and the gardens more elaborate. This was clearly a suburb of the wealthy. Nobles, even. At length, Intef and the fellow stopped. I crouched to hide behind a shrub in a nearby garden. They seemed to have a conversation with the fellow pointing towards a certain house and holding out his hand. Intef shook his head and made some reply. The fellow put his hands on his hips and seemed to grow angry.

I could hear nothing of what they said, although I could imagine it. The fellow probably said the house to which he pointed was where Tey and the unknown man lived. He wanted the gem now, but Intef wouldn't give it to him until he saw them with his own eyes.

The argument continued with the fellow growing more angry and Intef simply shrugging at him. At last, the fellow stomped away. I crept around the other side of the bush to keep out of sight while he passed. He muttered to himself as he walked. Once he was gone, I turned to see what Intef was doing and jumped when I found him standing right behind me.

"I followed you," I said, rather unnecessarily.

"I noticed."

"We thought he might try to double cross you. Sabu stayed to mind the donkeys."

Intef shot me a bemused look.

"And what did you intend to do if he was indeed double crossing me?" he asked.

"I have my dagger."

My tone was more defensive than I intended. I had saved him before, hadn't I? Perhaps not with my dagger, but nevertheless, I got him out of the underworld.

"Come," he said. "There is a better place to watch the house from further down the street."

He led me to where a stand of dom palm trees provided sufficient cover for us to hide in their midst without obscuring our view.

"Now what?" I asked.

"Now we wait." Intef sat with his back against a trunk. "Sit down so you are less visible. We may be here for a while."

I studied the house as we waited. It was very fine, almost a small palace. Certainly the kind of residence one might expect to be inhabited by a former queen. Many large windows with their shutters wide open to capture the breeze. An orderly garden with well-trimmed shrubs and beds that would likely provide an abundance of flowers during *shemu*. A wooden bench beneath a shady pavilion provided a pleasant place to sit and enjoy the garden. If my life had been different, I might have lived in such a home once I was no longer queen.

Inside the house, someone walked past a window, although I caught no more than a glimpse of a male figure.

"That is him," Intef whispered. "Ay."

"What do we do?" I asked.

"We wait. We need to know whether anyone else is in there before we act."

"What about Sabu? Should I go get him?"

"We may need him. I can manage Ay, but if anyone else is there, I will need help. Do you know the way back?"

"I think so."

But I had been focused on following Intef and assumed we would return to Sabu together. I hadn't watched for landmarks that would let me find my way back alone. Intef must have guessed.

"Stay here and watch Ay," he said. "I will go for Sabu."

"What do I do if he leaves? Should I follow him?"

"Just stay here. It doesn't matter if he goes out. If he lives here, he will return sooner or later. All you have to do is observe the house. We need to know how many other people are in there. Watch the doors and windows. Watch for anyone coming or going. As long as nobody has seen you, stay and watch."

"What do I do if somebody notices me?"

"Try to find your way back to where we were earlier. Just get as far as you can and wait. I will find you."

He slipped away, leaving me alone.

FORTY-ONE

Intef returned with Sabu long before I expected him. He must have run all the way there. They brought only a single pack each.

"We left a boy to watch the donkeys and the rest of the packs," Sabu said.

"What have you seen?" Intef asked as they sat beside me amongst the dom palms.

"Nothing new," I said. "Someone keeps walking past different windows. I never quite see him long enough to be sure, but I think it is always Ay. I haven't seen anyone else."

"So perhaps Tey and her family are out for the day," Intef said.

"Do we act now then?" Sabu asked. "If he is alone, this seems like a good time."

"We aren't certain he is alone," Intef said. "The house is large enough that other people could be inside without us seeing them from here. We also don't know whether they have any guards. They may well have a couple stationed inside."

"I will go watch from behind the house," Sabu said. "If there are others inside, I might see them from back there."

Intef nodded and Sabu left, circling around a couple of other houses as he went.

"You want to wait until night, don't you?" I asked Intef.

"Yes. Even though it will likely mean more people are inside, I'd rather wait until everyone is asleep and try to retrieve him under the cover of darkness."

"He will wake up, though. Surely he will make enough noise that everyone will know."

"We will gag him before he wakes," Intef said. "We will have to restrain him and the struggle might wake others, anyway. But I want to see who else lives here before deciding. I would like to know whether any of them have enough training to be a problem."

"But how will you know?"

"I just need to see them. A trained soldier is recognisable in the way he walks and the way he holds himself. Anyone else won't be a problem, not with Sabu here to help."

We waited through the afternoon and saw nothing other than more glimpses of Ay.

"Whatever is he doing?" I whispered. "He just walks from chamber to chamber."

"He is certainly restless," Intef said. "That could be a problem for us. It will be easier to snatch him if he is sleeping than if he is still up and wandering around."

An hour or so before dusk, six people approached from the far end of the street.

"This could be the queen's family," Intef said.

As they came closer, I recognised Tey. Her proud bearing was unmistakable even before I made out her face.

"There is Tey," I said, then realised my comment was probably unnecessary. Intef would have recognised her long before I did.

"I don't know any of the others," he said. "Do you?"

"I don't think so."

Beside Tey walked an elderly woman with white hair. She had a hunched back and used a cane to steady herself. Behind them were two younger women, perhaps aged around twelve years, and two boys who were young enough to be naked.

"No guards," I said.

"Hmm. If they have guards, it seems unlikely the women would go out for the day without them."

"Might the guards have stayed to watch Ay?"

"Possible, I suppose."

"But you think it unlikely."

"I do. If you have only one guard, what man would keep him at home to watch over himself instead of sending him with the women-folk? If they have more than one guard, he might keep one with him and send the other."

"Is it really possible he has no guards? He was Pharaoh, after all."

"He abdicated. No reasonable person would assume he has any influence over Horemheb, so what benefit is he to anyone?"

"What about riches? People would expect him to be a wealthy man. Wouldn't he want guards in case somebody breaks in and tries to rob him?"

"If he walked away without riches, he might not consider such a thing. I think we are safe to assume there are no guards inside."

As the sun set, somebody inside the big house closed the shutters and lit the lamps. Biting insects descended on us outside. I slapped them halfheartedly, but it seemed to make no difference to their numbers, and I resigned myself to being bitten. I spotted a shadowy figure making its way around the side of the house.

"Is that Sabu in the yard?" I asked.

"He has been checking the windows and trying to see inside."

Soon Sabu slipped across the street and came to where we hid.

"Ay is in there, along with seven other people. His wife and an elderly couple who look enough like her to assume they are her parents. One of them is the older woman who returned earlier. Also the two women who were with them and the two boys."

"No sign of husbands of the younger women?" Intef asked.

Sabu shook his head. "One of them must be the woman the fellow who showed you here wanted to marry. The boys are too young to belong to either Tey or her mother and too old to be sons of the younger women."

"There must be an older daughter," Intef said. "Perhaps one who has gone to the West."

"Why would the boys not be with her husband's family if that is the case?" I asked.

"Maybe he went to the West ahead of her and the family could not afford to care for them," Intef said with a shrug. "Maybe he had no family left, or there was no husband at all. It doesn't matter. The boys are too young to be a problem for us, other than that they might raise the alarm."

"They were running around playing when I looked in the windows," Sabu said. "They will tire themselves out and probably go to bed early."

"So we wait until everyone is asleep, then we go in and retrieve Ay," Intef said. "Our aim will be to get in and out without waking anyone else."

I settled myself more comfortably. My behind had gone numb and my feet tingled after sitting in the same spot all afternoon.

"Go for a walk," Intef said to me. "It is dark enough that nobody will notice. Don't go too far, though."

"I am fine."

If he could sit here all day without fidgeting, I could do the same.

We only had to wait an hour or two before the lamps went out, all except for one that someone carried from chamber to chamber.

"It must be Ay," Intef said.

For several hours, Ay continued to prowl the house.

"Does the man never sleep?" Sabu asked.

"Rest if you can," Intef said. "Both of you. I will wake you when he settles."

My eyes were heavy and I kept jerking awake as my head nodded. Sabu still looked alert and I didn't want to sleep if neither of them were, but I couldn't keep awake much longer. I would close my eyes for just a few minutes. It would be easier to stay awake once my eyes were more rested. I woke when Intef tapped my knee.

"I think he has gone to bed," he said. "Let's go."

I stumbled to my feet, not quite awake yet, and almost fell over. Sabu was already up. Intef waited another few minutes, likely to give me time to wake up properly, then gestured for us to go. He and Sabu both had their daggers in their hands. Before I could reach for mine, Intef handed me a coiled rope from his pack.

I stared down at it. He expected to tie Ay up to make him come with us. Obvious really, but I hadn't considered this. Even though Intef mentioned the possibility of tying Ay to a donkey, I had still pictured him walking with us, perhaps convinced to do so after being threatened, but walking on his own feet, nonetheless. For the first time, I considered the gravity of what we were about to do. We were going to kidnap a man from within his own home.

"We will go around the left side," Intef whispered. "The lamp went out around the second last window. We will see what we can see from the window, then find the nearest door."

"What if Tey is in the same chamber?" I asked.

This suddenly seemed like a bad idea. There were too many ways it might go wrong. Too many people to sound the alarm and send for help. Too many chances for us all to be arrested.

"She slept in her own chambers in the palace," Sabu said. "So she likely does here as well."

"Samun, if anything goes wrong, I want you to run, you hear me?" Intef said. "Go to Memphis. Horemheb will protect you."

"I won't leave you and Sabu," I said.

"If something goes wrong, you must. If you get away, then you can find a way to get us out of prison, but if you are arrested, you can do nothing for us. Understand?"

I didn't like the thought of deserting them, but if I was free, I could get Horemheb to intervene for Intef and Sabu if necessary. I draped the rope over my arm, then got my dagger out of my pouch. My hands only shook a little.

We darted across the street and pressed ourselves to the side of the house, waiting for any sign someone might have seen us. When we reached the window Intef had indicated, he stood to the side of it and peered in between the shutters. He gave us a shrug. I guessed he wasn't able to see anything inside.

Around the corner and about halfway along the house, we came to a door. Locked from the inside, of course. Intef set to work undoing the top hinge with his dagger and Sabu worked on the bottom one. In less than a minute, both hinges came off and they removed the door. They leaned it against the wall, followed by the bar that had secured it.

"Ready?" Intef whispered.

I nodded and clutched my dagger tighter, fearing the noise it would make if I dropped it.

We slipped into the house and waited in the first chamber while our eyes adjusted. It was much darker than outside in the moonlight and at first I could see nothing. Soon enough, though, I made out some shapes, even if I couldn't tell what they were. Intef gestured to us and we made our way along the hallway.

I tried to walk as quietly as possible, but even so, I was aware of the soft swish of my sandals against the mud brick floor. My breathing was shaky and far too loud. My heart pounded. Surely, if Ay was still awake, he would hear me coming. Intef took the rope from me and leaned close to whisper into my ear.

"Wait here and listen for anyone coming. He should be in the next chamber to the right."

Intef and Sabu continued down the hall, much more quietly than I had moved. They hesitated at the door, listening I presumed. After a few moments, they slipped inside. I heard brief sounds of a struggle, then all was quiet. Shortly afterwards, Sabu backed out into the hall. Intef followed and between them they carried Ay, who didn't appear to be resisting.

I hurried back to where we had taken the door from its hinges. They followed me out and we set off down the street. The moonlight was bright enough to see that Ay was not awake. They had tied a gag around his mouth and bound his hands.

"I had to knock him out," Intef said.

"He is alive?" I asked.

"Of course," he said. "But he wasn't going to come quietly, so I had no choice."

"Are you and Sabu able to carry him all the way to where we left the donkeys?"

"We won't need to. We just need to get him away from the house. Once he wakes up, he can walk."

Only another few minutes passed before Ay stirred and struggled.

He groaned and writhed until Intef and Sabu dropped him on the ground. He glared up at them.

"We are taking you to face justice for the murder of the Hittite prince." Intef's tone was curt. "You will walk on your own feet. If you give me any reason to, I will cut your throat myself and call it just punishment. Do you understand?"

Ay tried to speak, although the gag muffled his words. Intef kicked him in the ribs, not too gently.

"I did not ask whether you agree," he said. "I asked if you understood. It has been a long day and I am tired. We are charged with finding you, but frankly, if all I have to carry back is your head, that is fine with me. So which is it to be? Will you walk or shall I take your head and leave your body here for the jackals to find?"

Ay shook his head, still trying to talk.

"I will assume you are saying you intend to walk," Intef said.

Between him and Sabu, they hauled Ay to his feet. Sabu held his arms while Intef took another rope from his pack. He tied it around one of Ay's ankles and secured the other end around his own waist. A third rope secured Ay's other ankle to Sabu's waist. Unless Ay could free his hands and get a dagger to cut both ropes, he wouldn't be able to get away.

"Now you will walk," Intef said. "And you will keep up. If you fall over, we will drag you behind us."

We set off. Ay resisted, but when it became clear that Intef really didn't intend to wait for him, he began to walk.

FORTY-TWO

The streets were almost empty as we made our way back to the donkeys. A dog followed for a while, creeping through the shadows, and several cats darted across the road, but thankfully there were no people. Until we rounded a corner and came face to face with the young man who led Intef to Ay's house.

His face was flushed and he appeared less than steady on his feet. He glared at Intef.

"You," he said.

He didn't seem to notice our prisoner until Ay made a strangled noise. The fellow stopped, wobbled a little, and fixed his gaze on Ay. Ay held up his hands, showing the man he was bound, and tried to talk.

"Keep walking, friend," Intef said. "For your own safety, forget what you see here."

He pulled out the gem he had promised the fellow and offered it to him. The fellow looked from Intef to Ay, then to Sabu, then snatched up the gem and hurried away. Ay called after him, still trying to talk beneath his gag.

"Silence." Intef slapped Ay on the back of his head. "Unless you want me to knock you out again. I assume you would prefer to know what is happening."

We reached the donkeys and relief surged through me at the sight of the beasts and our packs, although the boy who was supposed to be minding them was nowhere to be seen. We got Ay on a donkey with some difficulty and another threat from Intef to take just his head with us. Once we had him tied firmly in place, we headed back to Rhakotis.

The sun peered over the horizon by the time we reached Rhakotis and made our way to where Suppiluliumas's army was camped. Despite the early hour, many of the soldiers were already out of bed, sharpening weapons and breaking their fast.

We tied the donkeys to a tree, then made our way through the army. Many a soldier stiffened and turn to watch as we passed, but nobody challenged us. I was surprised, but perhaps the presence of a man who was clearly a prisoner stopped them. It reminded me of what Intef once told me, that as long as you look like you are supposed to be there, most people won't try to stop you.

We weren't far from Suppiluliumas's tent before a soldier stepped in front of us.

"You can wait here," he said in Akkadian. "While I check whether he wishes to see you."

"We have brought the man responsible for his son's death," I said. "As he asked."

Four soldiers surrounded us while the first went to Suppiluliumas's pavilion. He quickly returned to usher us inside.

"No weapons," the soldier said as we reached the entrance.

We handed over our daggers. The soldier raised his eyebrows at taking a dagger from me, and I bristled.

Suppiluliumas was breaking his fast with some bread. His gaze went immediately to Ay, who was still bound and gagged.

I prostrated myself on the rug, and Intef and Sabu followed my example.

"Get down," a soldier growled at Ay.

I was surprised that so many of Suppiluliumas's soldiers spoke Akkadian. Ay tried to speak, and although the gag muffled his words, he sounded anything but penitent.

"I said, get down."

Without warning, the soldier slammed the hilt of his dagger between

Ay's shoulders, then kicked him in the back of the knees. Ay crumpled to the rug.

Suppiluliumas busied himself with finishing his meal and it was not until he had eaten the last crumb that he bid us rise.

"Remove the gag," he said.

The soldier held his dagger high and Ay flinched away from him.

"Stand still or I might accidentally slit your throat rather than cut off your gag," the soldier said.

Ay complied, although he made a noise that sounded like a whimper as the fellow sliced away the linen. As it fell from his face, he sucked in a deep breath.

"What is the meaning of this?" he cried in Akkadian. I had forgotten he would have been schooled in the language of diplomats. Even in his role as chief advisor, he would have needed to know Akkadian. "These criminals took me from my home in the middle of the night, bound and abducted, with no knowledge of where I was to be taken. I do not even know whether my wife and her family still live."

"Shut your mouth," Suppiluliumas said, his tone disinterested. He looked at me. "Is this the man who killed my son?"

"It is. This is Ay, the man who forged my signature on a marriage contract so he could steal the throne. Intef here was present when Ay learned of the approach of the Hittite party."

I gestured towards Intef and repeated my response in Egyptian. Intef gave a low bow and I translated his words for Suppiluliumas.

"This is the man who gave the order for Zannanza to be killed. He had received word that a small Hittite party approached the Egyptian border. We knew there were no more than five squads. They were detained while word was sent to Memphis. Pharaoh, as he was called then, was looking for an excuse to rid himself of my lady, Ankhesenamun, who was at that time the Queen of Egypt.

"He had thought that with her brother-husband's death, the queen would be more compliant, but he found that was not the case. He was unable to control her in the way he wanted and he desired to rid himself of her so he could rule on his own. When he received news of the Hittite party, he accused her of treason, of conspiring with an enemy to allow

Egypt to be invaded and the throne seized. He then ordered the Hittite party to be killed."

"I want to be very clear about what you are saying," Suppiluliumas said, when I finished relaying Intef's words. "This man standing before me, the one who is bound, was Pharaoh at the time my son was killed, yes?"

"Yes," I said, before translating for Intef and Sabu.

"And at the time he gave the order for my son to be killed, he knew that only fifty men accompanied him?"

"That is correct."

"He ordered my son and his men to be killed so he could claim we tried to invade Egypt, even though any man of sound mind would have known that fifty men were nothing more than an ambassadorial party?"

"Yes."

"I am nothing if I am not a fair man." Suppiluliumas directed his words to Ay now. "So I will allow you the opportunity to explain your actions. Tell me why you killed my son."

"I received word of a Hittite army approaching," Ay said. "Thousands upon thousands of men. I could think of no peaceful reason any country would send so great a number towards an ally. My captains had orders they were not to engage first, since Hattusa is an ally. They were only to defend us if provoked. If they could find a peaceful solution, they were to do so."

I scoffed, and Suppiluliumas shot me a look, a clear warning to be silent.

"When the Hittite army reached the Egyptian border, they attacked without warning or provocation," Ay continued. "I was told that a prince of the Hittites led the charge. My men defended their country as I had ordered them to do. I can find no fault with their actions, only with yours in sending an army."

"You would stand in front of me and lie to my face?" Suppiluliumas asked. "Do you think I don't know how many men I myself sent with my son?"

"I can only tell you what I was told, of the approach of a vast army."

"So when your men told you they had defeated my *vast army* of thousands of men, you believed them?" Suppululiumas said. "You did not question how the Egyptian army could have done that?"

"Of course not." Ay's voice was scornful. "Our army is the most skilled in the world. If my captains said they defeated an invading army, that they killed every last one of the attackers, I believed them. I rewarded them for their valour."

Surely he knew what kind of response his words would provoke.

"You rewarded the men who slaughtered my son and his escorts?" Suppiluliumas's voice was deathly quiet, as if he barely controlled his rage.

"Of course I did." Either Ay didn't realise how much he angered Suppiluliumas or he thought he could bluster his way through it. "And I take offence at your tone. You are all but accusing me of lying."

"I *am* accusing you of lying," Suppululiumas roared. "Do you think that what your men did was not witnessed? You think I don't have spies in your court? I know what happened that day. That you ordered Zannanza's death. That you knew exactly how many men travelled with him. Everything Ankhesenamun and her man here have said matches what my spy already told me."

"That is preposterous," Ay started, but Suppululiumas cut him off with a wordless roar of rage.

"I have heard your words and I find you guilty." Suppululiumas pulled a dagger from his waistband. "I sentence you to death for the murder of Zannanza, son of the Hittites."

Ay shook his head and tried to step back, but the rope binding him to Intef and Sabu was already stretched as far as it could go. He toppled over, falling backwards onto his behind.

"No," he cried. "They are the guilty ones. She is an abomination. She claimed the throne for herself. Twice! She tried to rule as pharaoh. Women should not—"

"Silence," Suppululiumas shouted over him. "My decision is made and it is final. As my son died on his knees with his hands bound, so shall you. Get him up."

He directed the last at two of his soldiers. They stepped forward to haul Ay onto his knees. He resisted, but they gripped him firmly by the shoulders.

Suppululiumas stood over Ay.

"As my son died, so do you."

He lashed out with his dagger and slashed it across Ay's throat.

Blood spurted, and Ay seemed to try to speak. For a few moments he swayed on his knees, then he fell. Blood seeped beneath him, soaking into the rich fibres of the rug.

"Toss him onto the rubbish pit."

Suppululiumas wiped his dagger on his own shirt before tucking it back into the leather band around his waist. If he noticed the blood splattered across his face and chest, he made no move to clean it off.

A soldier cut the ropes binding Ay to Intef and Sabu, then they carried him, face down and still dripping blood, out of the tent.

"Remove the rugs," Suppululiumas said. "I do not want to smell his foul stink a moment longer."

Servants rolled up the rugs. Intef, Sabu and I stood to the side while they laid out clean ones. Suppululiumas stood with his back to us and only once the servants retreated did he turn to face us.

"So," he said, eyeing each of us. "You have done as I asked. You have brought me the man who killed my son."

"Will you honour your words and call off the battle?" I asked. "We have no wish to fight the Hittites. Hattusa has long been a friend to Egypt, and you have been a friend to both my brother and my father."

Should I tell him of my dream in which I saw him on his deathbed? But I still didn't know what led to that moment, so the information wouldn't be useful, and he might think I was trying to threaten him.

"You have done all this and you are not even a queen," he said.

"I am still my father's daughter and I was raised to be of use to my pharaoh. I act in my father's memory to restore the friendship between Egypt and Hattusa."

Suppululiumas gave a great sigh and suddenly looked very weary.

"I accept your overtures of peace. I will order my army to retreat."

"Thank you." My words were heartfelt and I bowed from my waist. "Thank you, majesty."

"Go now," he said. "Take your men and leave. I am sure you understand if I say I have no wish to see your face again. I do not believe you were involved in plotting my son's death, or that you had any intention of such a thing when you asked for one of my sons, but you must realise I hold you partially responsible. Zannanza would never have travelled to Egypt had it not been for your impassioned plea. Had I not believed you would make my son pharaoh, that our two countries would forever be joined as one, I would not have sent him. You may not be directly responsible for his death, but you share some part of the blame."

"I understand," I said. "And for whatever it is worth to you, I sincerely apologise. I, too, feel the blame of having begged you to send your son. I am more sorry than I can ever say."

FORTY-THREE

Suppiluliumas gestured for us to leave. As we made our way back through the army, I tried to define my conflicted emotions. I wasn't sorry Ay had gone to the West, but he was pitiful in his last moments. Ay had never been kind to me and he was undoubtedly responsible for the poisoned arrow that killed my brother. He ordered the deaths of both Sadeh and Zannanza. He held me down in my bed and tried to get a child on me, although, thank Isis, when Setau was born I saw more of Intef in his face than Ay.

I had spent the last couple of years trying to atone for not standing up to him more. Not being stronger in those early years when I might have still had a chance of controlling the advisors. My failure to tell my brother how much I feared his advisors' growing influence and control. My mistake in allowing Sadeh to face them in my place.

I had spent a long time blaming Ay for who he was, but was it really his fault he wasn't the man I thought he should be? In a way, my father was just as much to blame. He allowed his advisors far too much freedom to do as they pleased. If he had taken a firmer hand with them, perhaps their corruption wouldn't have spread so far.

But that wasn't fair to my father, either. He acted as he thought best and he never did anything he believed would be detrimental to either his people or his country. He just didn't always see what was right in front of him, so focused as he was on his god and on his grief at the loss of my mother.

Perhaps in a way I had atoned for not just my failings, but also my father's. I had averted war with the Hittites, which would have been devastating to both Egypt and its people. It was not a bad outcome for a girl child who had been expected to do no more than forge a strategic alliance with marriage to one of Pharaoh's allies.

As we emerged from the crowd of the army, Sabu gestured towards the donkeys.

"I can go sell them," he said. "Unless you need me for something else?"

"Go on," Intef said. "I will walk for a while. I need to clear my head." He held out his hand to me. "Come with me?"

We wandered off, choosing a path along the shore away from the busyness of the dock. I took off my sandals and enjoyed the feeling of my toes sinking into the silky sand.

"It is done, is it not?" Intef asked.

I sighed, suddenly so tired I could barely find the strength to reply.

"You have removed Ay from the throne and resolved the threat of war with the Hittites," he said. "Those are the things you said you needed to do."

"Yes, it is done."

"So what now?"

"I could do with some breakfast," I said. "And I feel like I could sleep for a week."

"That is not what I meant. What do we do now? Where will we live?"

I stopped to look out to sea. The wind was in my face, pushing my hair back. I breathed deeply of the salty water. Somewhere out there was Crete, and Istnofret who had become my dearest friend. I loved Intef, but the thought of not having Istnofret in my life left me feeling empty.

"I think..." I paused to gather my thoughts and be certain before I spoke. This felt like something I couldn't take back once I said it. "I think I would like to go back to Crete. Live near Istnofret and Renni."

Intef laughed.

"I cannot say I am surprised," he said.

"Would you mind terribly? Could you bear to settle somewhere that is not Egypt?"

"As long as we are together, I don't care where we are. Renni is a good friend and I would be happy to be near him and Istnofret."

"What about you, Shadow?" I asked. "Could you be happy in Crete?"

Of course, my shadow didn't reply. I hadn't expected it to. Had only meant to let my shadow know I thought about its wellbeing and not just my own.

"That is what we will do then," I said. "There is nothing left for me in Egypt. There is nobody here I care about. If I can have you and Istnofret with me, I can be happy."

"What about your sisters? I thought you would want to look for them, but you know they won't still be in Crete."

I held my breath for a moment, testing my response. This, too, couldn't be changed once I said it.

"No," I said at last. "I swore they would be free to live their own lives the day you sent them away. I must hold to that. As much as I would love to find them, to see the women they have grown into, I need to let them be. They probably hate me anyway. I exiled them. Sent them away from everything they knew and loved. Made them outcasts. They would not wish to see me even if I could find them."

"We could send a message to Mutnodjmet to tell her we intend to settle in Crete. If your sisters decide to look for you one day, they would probably enquire at the palace."

"That is a good idea."

I stooped to snatch up a handful of sand and let it trickle between my fingers. The breeze caught the grains and scattered them as they fell.

"Have your dreams given you any clues about what may lie ahead now?" Intef asked.

"I knew I would speak with Suppiluliumas. He will either die shortly or meet a new babe, but I don't know what prompts either fate, and I have seen nothing that comes after that. I suppose what happened today has determined which fate he will face. Maybe now he will live to return home and father another child."

"Perhaps that signals the last of the big decisions you will need to make."

"Osiris hinted I could learn to control my dreams. I would like to go back to the old woman, the one who showed me the images in the bronze bowl. Maybe she can help me figure out how."

"Have you ever come to any conclusion about why you see these alternative fates in your dreams?" he asked.

I dug my toes through the sand as I tried to find an answer.

"I grew up knowing I would be expected to be useful to my Pharaoh," I said. "But I suppose the gods had other plans for me. Yes, they intended for me to be useful, but not by marrying a man Pharaoh wanted an alliance with. By averting the war, I have changed the course of history for my people. I am sure my father never intended anything like that when he told me I would be useful to him when I grew up."

"But how have the dreams helped you?" Intef asked. "You never know what will force either fate, and you've told me how the fate that seems most desirable never ends up being the best one. So what use are they?"

"Preparation, I think. Forewarning. I am not sure the gods ever intended me to strive towards one future or the other. I think they knew my life would have more impact than my father ever expected and the dreams were a way of warning me to be careful in what I did. That the consequences of my decisions would reach far beyond what I expected. Maybe that is why I never knew which decision would result in which fate. It didn't matter because it was never about changing the future. "

"It pleases me that you haven't dreamed of anything past today," he said. "Perhaps now it is time for you to live a normal life."

"For us to live a normal life," I said.

We were silent for some time after that, staring out to sea, each lost in our own thoughts. The further we got from the underworld, the less grey Intef looked. With time, perhaps, he would look like he had before.

I closed my eyes and let myself enjoy the breeze in my hair. I still didn't like watching the waves. They called me, but perhaps not as strongly as they once did. Maybe that had been because of the memory of when I drowned trying to surface in my mind.

During my purification ceremony, Isis said the one was not ready. Behenu had suggested the one was me, but I hadn't believed her. Now I knew she was right. It must have been me. But what was it Isis had thought I wasn't ready for?

A girl child. A princess, and not even the eldest. Destined for no more than a strategic alliance. An important marriage. Words I could say long before I understood their meaning. And yet the decisions I made would shape the course of history for my people. Everything I had endured had prepared me for this.

Our vast journey across the world and into the underworld. The loss of my son, Setau, and the decision to give up my daughter, Meketaten, in exchange for the Eye of Horus. Being the one to decide we should cut off Intef's arm to save his life. Claiming the throne twice and giving it up both times. Having my heart ripped from my chest while I still lived and facing judgement in the Hall of Osiris. These things taught me strength. Leadership. The importance of truth, and of friendship.

They prepared me for the day when I would be forced to take responsibility for my actions which had nearly led to war with the Hittites. Perhaps this was what Isis meant when she said I wasn't ready. Without enduring everything I had, I couldn't have made the decisions I did.

Without being stripped of my identity as Queen of Egypt and Great Royal Wife, I wouldn't have offered my life to save ten thousand Egyptian children.

Without the grief of losing two children myself, I wouldn't have understood Suppiluliumas's need to exact vengeance for the wrongful death of his son.

If I was still wrapped up in my identity and my status and my power, I never could have averted the war which would have decimated my country. I changed the future after all, even if that wasn't what the gods had intended. I had steered my country towards peace.

What would my father think if he knew what I had done? Would he be proud of his girl child who was only ever supposed to marry a man who would be useful to Pharaoh?

"Your father would be proud of you," Intef said, as if he knew what I was thinking.

I looked up to the sky, even though I knew my father's star wouldn't be visible yet.

"I hope you were watching, Father," I whispered. "I hope you know what I did. I made a strategic alliance, just like you always said I would."

The wind changed direction, blowing my hair over my face. As I pushed it away, the sun caught my finger ring, making it sparkle. I held up my hand to study it. It was a band of gold inlaid with a circle of lapis lazuli, the ring Behenu found in my chambers after we returned to Memphis. At the time I had been pleased that at least one thing from my former life had survived, despite how hard they tried to erase all memory of me.

I pulled the ring off my finger. It was the last thing I had left from my old life which was mine alone. The last thing that signified my status as Queen of Egypt, Great Royal Wife, Lady of the Two Lands. Great of Praises, Sweet of Love, Mistress of Upper and Lower Egypt. They were all titles I clung fiercely to at one point. I barely recognised that woman any more. She wasn't me, and I didn't need this reminder of her.

I drew back my arm and threw the ring as hard as I could. Sunlight glinted as it arced over the water and sank beneath the surface of the waves.

"Let's go home to Crete," I said to Intef.

FORTY-FOUR

My dear Shala

I am sorry it has taken so long for me to write to you. It is only in recent weeks that we have stopped travelling and have made a home for ourselves on the island of Crete. I think fondly of our time in Babylon with you and Belasi. If we had not met you, and Belasi had not taken us to the archives, we would never have found the clue that led us to the artefact we were looking for.

I remember how much you loved to learn stories from other places and peoples. I have many stories to share with you, but they can wait for another day. For now, there is one story I want to tell you.

There was once a girl who was born in the underworld. Legend says that a child born in the underworld can never leave, so the girl had to stay there when her parents returned to the world of mortals.

She was given to one of the guardians of the underworld, to live with them and to train to one day replace them in their sacred duty as a guardian of the gate. Her role would be to see that mortals who found themselves in the underworld passed safely through the gates and back to their own world, and to stop any creatures of the underworld from leaving through the same pathway.

Time neither passes nor not passes in the underworld. The girl grew up anyway, since she was of mortal parents and that is what mortal children do, but after some time there, she was no longer fully human. One day, she might be a goddess. One day, there might be other stories told of her.

But for now, she trains to be a guardian and the only people who know about her are her parents and those who travelled with them. They will tell the story of the guardian of the underworld. They will remember her. I hope that in sharing her story with you, Shala, you will pass it on, so others know of the girl who was born in the underworld and who can never leave.

I remain your friend
  Ankhesenamun

If you enjoyed Ankhesenamun's journey, you might like The Amarna Princesses series. The journey begins with *Outcast*.

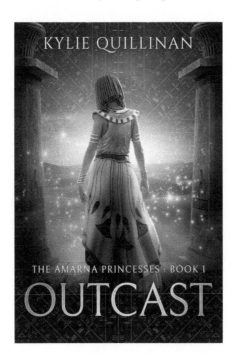

AUTHOR'S NOTE

As Ankhesenamun's journey draws to an end, I find myself at a loss. I've lived with Samun and her friends for so long that I don't quite know what my life will be without them. I hear her voice in my head, I see snippets of her life as I fall asleep. I've dreamed about her more times than I can count. I'm not sure I will ever again write a character who sinks so deeply into my soul. She has left a lasting influence on my life, this woman we know so very little about.

So, as one series ends and another begins, this is a moment to pause and thank those who supported me through these last six books.

The readers who have come with Ankhesenamun and me on this journey.

Neal, who knows better than anyone how difficult it can be to live with a writer.

My precious dogs, who faithfully guarded me while I wrote: Muffin, Bella, Lulu, Molly. The faces have changed through the years, but the comforting presence of a snoring dog is constant.

My parents, Murray and Suzanne, who have enthusiastically supported each new instalment.

My editor, Mary Novak, and her difficult suggestions which always make the story stronger.

The team at Deranged Doctor Design who have produced another series of striking covers for me.

My narrator, Catherine Bilson, who has done a tremendous job with the audiobooks of this series.

The makers of my favourite gin, without which these books would probably never have been finished.

I hope you will join me on another journey now as I pick up the story of Tey and the sisters Ankhesenamun sent away from Egypt.

Kylie Quillinan

May 2022

ALSO BY KYLIE QUILLINAN

The Amarna Age Series

Book One: *Queen of Egypt*

Book Two: *Son of the Hittites*

Book Three: *Eye of Horus*

Book Four: *Gates of Anubis*

Book Five: *Lady of the Two Lands*

Book Six: *Guardian of the Underworld*

Daughter of the Sun: An Amarna Age Novella

The Amarna Princesses Series

Book One: *Outcast*

Book Two: *Catalyst*

Book Three: *Warrior*

See kyliequillinan.com for more books, including exclusive collections, and newsletter sign up.

ABOUT THE AUTHOR

Kylie writes about women who defy society's expectations. Her novels are for readers who like fantasy with a basis in history or mythology. Her interests include Dr Who, jellyfish and cocktails. She needs to get fit before the zombies come.

Her other interests include canine nutrition, jellyfish and zombies. She blames the disheveled state of her house on her dogs, but she really just hates to clean.

Swan – the epilogue to the Tales of Silver Downs series – is available exclusively to her newsletter subscribers. Sign up at kyliequillinan.com.

Lightning Source UK Ltd.
Milton Keynes UK
UKHW012021010722
405272UK00002B/30